SUNNY SWEET
Is SO Dead Meat

Also by Jennifer Ann Mann

Sunny Sweet Is So Not Sorry

SUNNY SWEET
Is SO Dead Meat

Jennifer Ann Mann

illustrated by Jana Christy

BLOOMSBURY
NEW YORK   LONDON   NEW DELHI   SYDNEY

First published in the United States of America in May 2014
by Bloomsbury Children's Books
www.bloomsbury.com

Bloomsbury is a registered trademark of Bloomsbury Publishing Plc

For information about permission to reproduce selections from this book, write to
Permissions, Bloomsbury Children's Books, 1385 Broadway, New York, NY 10018
Bloomsbury books may be purchased for business or promotional use. For information on
bulk purchases please contact Macmillan Corporate and Premium Sales Department at
specialmarkets@macmillan.com

Library of Congress Cataloging-in-Publication Data
Mann, Jennifer Ann.
Sunny Sweet is so dead meat / by Jennifer Ann Mann.
pages   cm
Summary: When Sunny Sweet, age six, devises a science experiment that requires her big
sister, Masha, to look weird all day, Masha will try almost anything to get them home from
the science fair without causing a scene.
ISBN 978-1-59990-978-3 (hardcover) • ISBN 978-1-61963-233-2 (e-book)
[1. Sisters—Fiction.   2. Genius—Fiction.   3. Science fairs—Fiction.
4. Schools—Fiction.   5. Single-parent families—Fiction.   6. Russian
Americans—Fiction.   7. Adventure and adventurers—Fiction.]   I. Title.
PZ7.M31433Sq 2014   [Fic]—dc23   2013038028

Book design by John Candell
Typeset by Westchester Book Composition
Printed and bound in the U.S.A. by Thomson-Shore Inc., Dexter, Michigan
2 4 6 8 10 9 7 5 3 1

All papers used by Bloomsbury Publishing, Inc., are natural, recyclable products
made from wood grown in well-managed forests. The manufacturing processes
conform to the environmental regulations of the country of origin.

To my sister Christine Carpenter

SUNNY SWEET
Is SO Dead Meat

Sunny Sweet Is So Dead Meat

There is something kind of spooky about a school on a Saturday. And it's twice as spooky when it's a school you don't know.

"Are we early?" I asked my little sister. There didn't seem to be any cars in the parking lot except for my mom's car . . . leaving.

"I needed to get here first," Sunny said. "So I told Mommy that the science fair started at ten. It actually starts at eleven."

"Really, Sunny?" I groaned. "I already have to waste an entire Saturday doing this with you. I could have totally been at the hospital today hanging out with Alice." My friend Alice has spina bifida, which means that her spine didn't grow right before she was born. She sometimes has to be in the hospital for a few weeks at a time so the doctors can keep an eye on it.

Sunny's skinny little shoulders drooped, making me feel instantly bad.

"Anyway," I said, bumping her gently with my arm. "Maybe we can visit Alice tonight. They have late visiting hours on Saturday. And hey, I know," I added, "we can bring the trophy you're gonna win today to show her."

Sunny had won the trophy last year at our old school. In fact, Sunny always won the trophy wherever she went. I guess it was hard not giving the award to a scrawny little six-year-old kid with a brain that weighed more than the rest of her body put together.

"Okay, Masha," she said, beaming up at me from under the wide brim of her rain hat. It was my mother's hat, so it was way too big for her. It came down right to the top of her eyelashes. The rain jacket she wore was also my mother's, and it scraped at the pavement of the parking lot as we walked. Looking at her in this crazy rain outfit on this beautiful cloudless spring day, it hit me that I had no idea what her science experiment was about. Sunny was always working on a million different "projects," as she called them, and none of them made any sense to me. But her strange outfit was kind of interesting.

"What's your experiment about anyway?" I asked.

"It's about people who don't follow the rules of society."

"About what?"

Sunny stopped walking. "It's an experiment about being different," she said slowly. "Like, for example, at school. You know how some kids fit in and some kids don't?"

"Um, yeah," I said, surprised that I really did know. "So you're wearing a rain hat and raincoat on a beautiful sunshiny day because you're being different?" I asked.

"Good question," she said, putting down the box filled with her experiment in the middle of the parking lot.

I shook my head thoughtfully as if I were completely used to asking good questions. I had lived on this earth for almost double the number of years that Sunny had, but most days I felt like I'd only managed to develop half of the brain power.

"We have to do something before we go in," she said. "It's part of my experiment." She knelt down and started digging in her box. She found what she was searching for and pulled it out. "Here!" she said, jumping to her feet and handing it to me.

"Okay," I said. "It's a bottle of ketchup."

"Open it," she commanded, her eyes glowing.

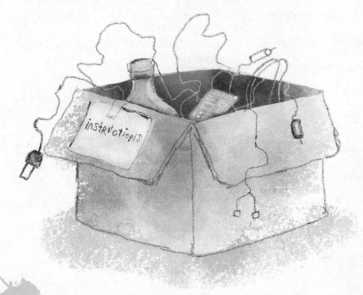

I put down the box of stuff that I'd been carrying for her and reached for the bottle. I began to open it. "Why can't we do this in the . . ."

There was a loud *pop!*

The top of the ketchup bottle exploded off. I stood there wet and stunned. I looked down at Sunny. Her rain gear was covered in ketchup. I looked down at myself. Ketchup was splashed across my T-shirt and jeans in giant blobs and streamed down my face and neck in ketchupy gobs.

"Oh my gosh," I breathed. "Sunny, are you okay?" I wiped at the ketchup on her coat, but it didn't smear. In fact, it just stayed there. "Holy mother of peanuts!" I wiped at the ketchup on my arm. It also stayed. "Why isn't this coming off?"

"It's not going to come off," she said excitedly. "It's a special red dye I invented."

"What?"

"Well, it will, but not for a few days. It has to wear off."

"*What?* You mean you did this on purpose?"

She nodded her head, smiling, happy that I had

5

finally gotten it. "Yes, Masha. You see, *you* are the one being different. You will walk around the science fair covered in weird red blotches, and I will observe how people react to you. *You're my science experiment!*"

Sunny unsnapped the rain jacket and stuffed it into her box. Her skirt and T-shirt were spotless. "Okay," she said. "Let's go."

"Let's go?" I said. I was standing in some random school's parking lot a million miles from home covered from head to toe in "weird red blotches." I could feel the anger gurgling up inside me. I guess Sunny could feel it too, because she took a slow step away from me.

I lunged . . . but that tiny little twig body of hers was too quick, and she took off toward the front doors of the building.

"SUNNY SWEET," I screamed, "YOU ARE SO DEAD MEAT!"

Being the Experiment

Before Sunny got to the front doors, she veered off into the grass toward a small group of trees. I was just about to grab her when she scampered up into one of the trees like a squirrel. I jumped after her with all my might but missed. And when I fell back to earth, all I had was one of her rain boots. Without thinking, I heaved the rain boot as hard as I could. It landed on the top of a little overhang that shaded the front entrance of the school.

"Look what you made me do!" I screamed.

I could see her spooky blue eyes peering at me from behind a branch filled with leaves.

"Sunny, get down here!"

She squirmed around on the branch, and then she reached into her pocket.

"Don't you dare," I growled.

There was a white flash of paper.

"Sunny Sweet, if you start taking notes on me like I'm some sort of white rat in a cage I'm going to rip your little head off."

I sucked in my breath as I watched her pull a pencil from her pocket.

"SUNNY!" I screamed, falling to my knees. I *was* some sort of rat. And I *was* in a cage. Only it was a cage that no one else ever saw. And because it was invisible to the world, it made me look like I was absolutely crazy. Anyone watching our fight would see a skinny little six-year-old kid running away from her big sister and hiding out in a tree. And then they'd see the big sister take her little sister's boot and hike it up onto the roof of a building while she screamed like a lunatic. They wouldn't see what was really happening!

There was a flash of moving metal. A car was pulling into the lot. *People were coming.*

"Sunny," I said, trying to sound calm. "Get out of the tree. Someone just pulled in."

The leaves rustled a bit, like she was getting comfortable—not like she was climbing down. I knew exactly what the scrawny mad scientist was going to do. She was going to *observe*.

Car doors opened and voices floated toward us.

"If you think I'm going to stand under this tree and wait for these people to come by so they can laugh at me covered in ketchup or dye or whatever the heck this is while you sit up in that stupid tree and take notes, guess what? I'm not." I looked around for someplace to hide. I took off running under the trees and around the corner of the building.

The school sat next to a rocky hill. There were only a few feet between the brick of the building and the rock of the hill. It was shady and a little cold. I peeked back around the corner. We had left Sunny's boxes sitting in the middle of the parking lot, and now two little kids were digging around in them. One of the little kids ripped off an envelope stuck to the side of the box and opened it.

"Don't touch that stuff," the lady with them said.

She walked over and looked down her nose into the boxes. The kid handed her what was in the envelope. It was probably some notes about Sunny's project. The woman read it and then looked up, searching the parking lot.

Another two cars pulled in. And then a third.

The lady took one last look around and then told the kids to pick up the boxes and follow her. I made a move to go for the boxes but then stopped. Who cared what might happen to Sunny's experiment? I wasn't going to expose myself for her science junk. The lady walked toward the front doors right under Sunny in her tree. A buzzer or bell went off. The lady must have pushed a doorbell on the school. There was an echoing click as the front door opened, and I heard the voices of the lady and a man as the door shut behind them.

I pulled out my phone. For one split second I thought about calling my mom. But there was no way that I was going to interrupt her at her painting class today. I just couldn't. She hadn't set up her canvas once since the three of us had left my dad in Pennsylvania and moved to New Jersey after the divorce. And this morning when she walked into the kitchen with her portfolio bag in her hand she was smiling that kind of smile that you can't stop smiling even if you try. Plus, if I called her, then she'd think that I couldn't handle myself and maybe not let me take the bus alone to see Alice anymore. I dialed Sunny.

I could hear her ringtone coming from up in the tree. It's the sound of an airplane taking off . . . or

x

11

landing. Every single time her phone rings she asks me which it is. I remind her that I do not care. But Sunny never listens and has to explain it. "Airplanes generate a higher noise level at takeoff than they do at landing, blah, blah, blah." I'm probably the only eleven-year-old in the world who knows this useless piece of information. And because of stupid stuff like this that Sunny shoves into my head every day of my life, other important stuff, like the lyrics to a cool song, falls right out the other side. There is only so much room in there.

"Hello, this is Sunny Sweet," she answered, as if she were the secretary picking up the phone for the tree.

"Get down," I spat into my cell. "We're going home right now."

I hadn't really thought about what I was going to yell at Sunny when I called her, but going home was exactly the right thing. I felt happy with my decision. Forget the science fair. We were going home.

More cars pulled into the parking lot.

"How are we gonna get there?" Sunny asked.

"The bus. Just like we were supposed to do after the fair was over."

"It's a Saturday. There are going to be a lot of people on the bus," she said.

"So."

"So how does that make you feel?"

"What are you talking about?"

"You know, how does it make you feel when you think about riding the bus in your current state?" I could actually hear the pages in her little notebook shuffling.

"MY CURRENT STATE," I screamed, "is now officially *loco*. So you better keep your skinny little butt up in that tree FOR-STINKIN'-EVER!"

I hung up. And then I plopped down in the grass and leaned back against the rocky hill, panting. I couldn't believe she did this to me. But then again, I guess I could believe it. Less than two weeks ago Sunny Sweet glued ten million plastic flowers in my hair as I slept, and that time I ended up at the hospital, where I had to have my head shaved. And not only that, but by accident the hospital put a cast on my arm because they thought I broke it when I didn't, so I also had a fake broken arm. Although I loved my fake broken arm.

I laid my arm in the beautiful orange cast on my lap. It was filled with the signatures of everyone in my class at school. They were all covered with red blotches! I found Junchao's name. Junchao Tao had been the first to sign my cast because she sat right behind me. Her tiny signature had a big red blob right over the top of it. I ran my fingers over the names on my cast. The dye had dried completely now. Thank goodness that my favorite signature, Michael Capezzi's, was not stained. His scratchy name was surrounded by red splatter, but none had fallen directly on it. I met Michael Capezzi at the hospital. He was there to get a brain tumor taken out of his head. After I got my head shaved, Michael helped Sunny and me get home from the hospital by helping us sneak on the bus. He and Alice signed in purple because they were both at the hospital and signed with the same marker. Alice's name was written in giant letters and was covered in splashes of red, just like the rest of me.

My T-shirt, my jeans, my sneakers, my hands, my arms . . . all of it was covered in red. I pulled my slouchy knit hat off my bald head. It was covered in red but it was a red hat, so you couldn't tell that much. I was sure my face was covered in red too.

I noticed a window down along the wall of the building. I put my hat back on and pulled myself up

from the cold grass to see if I could find out what my face looked like. I looked in. The room was dark so I couldn't see much more than the shadowy outline of my body. I seemed much taller and wider in the window. And where was my hat? I wasn't wearing it. I reached up to touch my head, but my reflection in the window didn't move. Then it did move. It opened the window and shouted at me.

"What are you doing sneaking around out there?"

I stumbled backward against the rock cliff. It was a janitor. Tripping sideways over my own sneakers, I scrambled toward the corner of the building and then out into the sunshine.

I was now in full view of the world. There were people everywhere. I tried to curl myself up into a human ball so I was smaller somehow, and less noticeable. I even tiptoed across the grass, hoping it would help make me more invisible. Sunny's words rang in my ears. *Your current state . . .* My teeth locked in my mouth and my shoulders pulled themselves right up to my ears. I was going to go get Sunny Sweet out of that tree and get on the bus and go *home*.

As I started toward the tree containing the Sunny-sized dark blob, something about the blob caught my eye—a flash of glass? I opened my eyes wide and stared hard. And then I saw her . . . sitting in the tree with a pair of binoculars focused right on me! I was like some sort of wild animal that she was watching on a safari.

"SUNNNNNNYYYYY!" I roared with all my might.

Everyone in the parking lot stopped. Car doors remained opened, kids froze mid-run, parents stared openmouthed, even the breeze stopped blowing, and the clouds paused in the sky.

It was confirmed. I was a complete loser.

Then the world shrugged at the broken-armed crazy girl covered in ketchup shouting at a tree. They began to move again, although they all made sure to move as far away from me as possible. I was left with my face burning and my blood racing hot under my skin.

Exhausted, I flopped down on the grass and squeezed my eyes shut and tried to imagine myself at home . . . home, home, home . . . beautiful, wonderful home. Home in my shower, scrubbing this junk off me. But instead, I couldn't get the vision of the mini-monster out of my head, sitting happily in her tree and scribbling away in her little notebook about me. What did she say? *"You're my science experiment!"* And I was. She was right. Why was she always right?

My phone rang.

QUACK . . . QUACK, QUACK, QUACK.

Unfortunately, my ringtone was of a duck quacking. Sunny had put it on my phone last weekend when I was babysitting her and fell asleep over my math homework. Of course she'd told me the kind of duck it was and even what the duck was saying. Only Sunny would think she knew what a duck was talking about! Anyway, I meant to change it but kept forgetting. I snapped on my phone.

"Sunny Sweet, you are so dead meat!"

"What did she do this time?"

"Alice!" I sighed.

Instantly everything felt better.

What Is Normal?

I have ketchup all over me!"

"Are you in a diner?"

"A diner? What are you talking about?"

"What are *you* talking about?"

We laughed. I rolled over in the grass onto my back and let the sun shine down on my red-speckled face.

"Tell me about the ketchup," she said.

I took a breath and spoke slowly. "She exploded a ketchup bottle of red dye all over me that can't be washed off. And now I'm covered in red junk, lying on the front lawn of some stupid school!"

"What about your cast?"

"It's covered too."

"And Michael's signature?"

"That's okay, no red got on it."

I heard her sigh. "Where's Sunny? Is she with you?"

"Kind of," I said, glancing up at the dark blob in the tree.

"Kind of?"

"Well, she's up in a tree. But the tree is near me."

"What?"

"After Sunny exploded the ketchup bottle all over me, I chased her up a tree." I moaned.

"She exploded the bottle? Did she mean to do it?"

"Of course she meant to do it!" I shouted. "And don't tell me to calm down, please, Alice. It will kill me."

I heard her giggling.

"You can't laugh either."

"Okay, you can't tell me that you're sitting covered in ketchup at some random school with your little sister up in a tree and tell me not to laugh," she said. "Why did she do it? Is she covered in ketchup too?"

"No! Of course she isn't covered in ketchup! She's high and dry and looking completely normal, or rather as normal as she can look. She did it so that I don't look normal. I was supposed to be her science project at the science fair today. She thought she could cover me in red ketchup dye and follow me around the science fair taking notes while people laughed at me!"

"What kind of experiment is that?"

"I don't know. Sunny said something about not following the rules and being different," I mumbled.

"I'm googling it," she said.

I watched the clouds slide across the sky as the sun warmed my face. But after a few minutes of listening to Alice breathing into the phone while she researched, I got bored. I rolled onto my side and began collecting tiny little pebbles from the edge of the parking lot and lining them up in the shape of hearts. I could hear Alice laugh or snort every now and then as she read up on the mess I was in. I had made four pebble hearts and was working on the fifth when Alice finally

finished with her
research.

"Your sister
is nuts," she
said, laughing.

"Thanks, I
know."

"It looks like
she wants you to act weird so she can record how
people react to your weirdness."

"Ugh," I growled. "Why didn't she just walk around
and take notes on herself then?"

"Maybe the only way to get Sunny back is by acting normal," Alice said.

"I am acting normal!"

"You chased her up a tree."

I thought about Sunny's rain boot on the roof of
the building. I didn't mention it to Alice. It wouldn't
help my case. "If you were stranded at some school
with red dye exploded all over you, you would have
popped a wheelie in that chair of yours and chased
her right up a tree too!"

Alice's legs didn't work so she had to be in a wheel-chair.

"I can't pop a wheelie, Masha Sweet."

"You just haven't tried," I said.

"I love being your friend," she laughed.

"I love being your friend too. But right now all I want is to get home. Will you help me?"

"Of course. So, let's think. Why would someone normally be covered in red dye?"

"What?"

"You know, if Sunny wants you to look and behave like an insane person, you have to act like a sane person. What kind of sane person is covered in red dye?"

"You're a genius, Alice. Okay, how about it's blood and I'm a doctor."

"Surgeons don't walk out of surgery covered in their patients' blood and then take the bus home."

"Good point."

"How about you're an artist?" she said. "The red can be paint and you just got done with an art project."

"Yes! Great, Alice! Okay, I'm a painter." I stood up and wiped the pebbles and dust off my T-shirt and jeans and checked myself out. "Too bad I didn't wear my overalls today."

"You have overalls?"

"Yes. Don't you?"

"No. No one wears overalls."

"Painters wear overalls."

"You're an artist, not a painter. A painter paints a house, and you're only eleven years old. No one is going to think you are painting a house. So, artist, all you need are some paintbrushes and maybe a can of paint. Go into the school and find the art department. You can stick a couple of brushes in your pocket and carry the paint. That way, when you get on the bus to get home, no one will even think twice. *Voilà*, you're normal!"

"I love the way you think, Alice Rottersdam!"

She giggled. "Oh, I wish I could see you right now."

"Hold on," I told her. I held the phone as far away from myself as I could and snapped a picture and texted it over. I heard her honking laughter without even putting the phone to my ear.

"It's not that funny," I told her.

"It's hilarious!" she screeched. "Come to the hospital before you go home. Pleeease," she begged.

"No stinkin' way! I'm going to find me a paintbrush and some paint, and then I'm going to drag my little sister onto a bus and go directly home!"

"Remember, Sunny wants you to behave like a crazy person. So whatever you do, *be normal*."

"I hope I can do it," I said, breathing in deep. "It isn't going to be easy."

"Text me when you get home."

"Okay," I said. "Here I go."

"Be normal!" she shouted as I ended the call.

The Modern Artist
or an Artist Who
Paints Otters

I began to walk slowly toward the front doors of
the school. This was normal. People walked toward
doors. My heart thumped, and I tried to take a couple
of breaths to slow it down. Heart thumping as you
approach a door is not normal.

I took a quick look around. It was pretty quiet.
Everyone was inside the school for the fair, and so far
my normal walk to the front doors was uneventful. But
then I tripped, and my heart started back up again,
banging even harder. "Tripping is normal," I explained
to my stupid heart. "I trip all the time." It quieted down.

Passing "the tree," I had this urge to pick up a rock and pitch it at the dark blob scribbling away in its notebook, but throwing rocks at your little sister in hopes of knocking her out of a tree was not normal.

"Hi, Masha," Sunny said as I walked under her. She was still wearing the rain hat.

"Hi, Sunny," I answered in a highly normal way.

"Are you feeling better after your initial breakdown?" she asked.

My fingers itched for the rock, but I kept walking.

Once I got inside the school I moved to the shadows and leaned next to a fire extinguisher. I could hear the faint rumble of a crowd. Then I remembered something great . . . My friend Junchao was part of that crowd! I pulled out my cell phone and texted her that I was in the school and needed her help. Then I slid to the floor and waited for her to come save me. Junchao and I would find the art department and I'd "borrow" some art supplies and then I'd be on my way home!

I waited . . . and waited. My phone buzzed. I jumped a little, clicking it on. It was a text from Sunny.

Where are you?

Stay in your tree, I texted back.

I called Junchao. The phone rang and rang. Then it went to voice mail. Where was she? *I guess I'll have to find my own paint can and paintbrushes. Now if I were an art department, where would I be?* I decided to take the hallway leading away from the crowd sounds.

The hall was empty except for some paper scraps and that nose-stinging cleaning smell that school hallways always have. I peeked in every door as I went, but they were all just regular classrooms, not art rooms. I passed a girls' bathroom and thought about trying to wash this junk off. But then I remembered Sunny's words, *It's not going to come off. It's a special red dye I invented.* And I knew that it wouldn't work. So I kept going.

My phone buzzed with another text. Junchao! But it wasn't. It was my mom.

In my class. How is the fair?

Great, I typed. But then I erased it. Too happy. She'd suspect that something was wrong. Very science-y, I texted back instead. She sent me a smiley face.

I started back down the hall. I was almost to the

end of it when I heard the squeaking of running sneakers. I swung around in a circle searching for a place to hide. It was too late. Two little kids ran down the hall chasing each other. The first one ran right past me without even glancing my way. I think he was wearing a cape. The second one was definitely wearing a cape and a mask. When the second one got five feet past me, he stopped like a car throwing on its brakes at a red light.

"Is that blood?" he asked. "Are you in trouble? BATMAN!" He hollered down the hall so loudly that it almost knocked my hat right off my head.

He was wearing a red T-shirt with the letter *R* drawn on the front with a black Magic Marker. Around his neck was a yellow bath towel held together under his chin by a rubber band. His cheeks were bright red underneath his black mask from running around.

"No, I'm not in trouble," I said. "I'm an artist. It's paint."

The other little kid made it all the way down the hall before he realized he was no longer being

followed. He ran back toward us and stopped by sliding into us, nearly knocking us over. He was wearing
a gray T-shirt with a black bat drawn on it and a black
Halloween-costume cape around his shoulders. He

had on a winter mask/hat with two triangle felt ears glued to the top of it. They were obviously supposed to be Batman and Robin.

"Cool, blood!" he said.

"It's paint," Robin explained. "She's an artist."

Batman looked disappointed. "Why is there paint all over you?" he asked.

"I'm a modern artist," I told them.

"You're an otter artist?" asked Robin. "I love otters."

"A modern artist . . . modern," I said slowly. "Modern art just means you get to throw paint around."

"I love to throw stuff," whispered Batman from behind his mask. Lips always look so funny when they're under a mask, like they're bigger than they should be, and too important. Whether they thought I painted otters or threw stuff around, I could tell that I just became very interesting to them. Maybe this meant that they would help me. "Do you guys know where the art department is here? I'm new."

"Are you lost?" asked Robin, stepping so close that he was on my foot.

"We can help," cried Batman, pumping his fist in the air.

"Um," I said.

"Come on," said Batman, and he took off, cape flying. Robin followed. And because I had no better way of finding my props . . . so did I.

We ran through a few darkish hallways. I could hear the science fair off in the distance, but we didn't pass anyone, and we didn't get close to it.

We finally stopped at a big door at the end of a hall. "Is this it?" I asked, huffing.

"Yep," answered Robin. "Our dad is the math teacher here, so I know where everything is."

"My dad is . . . ," I started. But then I stopped. My dad was the principal of my old school. I used to know where everything was once too. Sometimes I forgot that I didn't live in Pennsylvania anymore and that we didn't live with my dad anymore.

"Our dad's not the math teacher!" Batman said. "Our dad and mom got killed by bad guys." Then he shoved the other half of the Dynamic Duo. "Right, Robin?"

"Don't push me," Robin whined.

"And," Batman added, stepping in front of Robin, "we know where everything is in this school because we're superheroes."

Robin gave Batman a shove.

Batman turned around and whacked Robin in the head.

"Cut it out, you two," I said. "Someone will come. Let's go." I tried the door and then let out a long sigh. It was locked. Alice's simple idea of looking normal wasn't feeling so simple right now. I pulled out my phone to see if Junchao had gotten back to me. She hadn't. I knew she was supposed to be here today. She was presenting some experiment on outer space or something. Why wasn't she answering me?

"Why do you care if someone comes, anyway? Is a bad guy after you?" asked Batman.

"Maybe she's the bad guy!" said Robin, his eyes filling up the tiny holes in his mask.

"I'm not a bad guy," I said.

"You look like a bad guy," said Robin.

"No, I don't."

"Do too. Good guys aren't splashed with red stuff," said Robin. "Only bad guys are. You look like the Joker."

"I look like . . ." I looked down at myself, but I couldn't come up with anybody that looked like me. So I repeated my only defense. "I'm not a bad guy."

"Yes, you are. You're a bad guy!" Robin put up both his fists in front of his face, getting ready to box me or something.

"Wait a minute. I'm the one who knows who the bad guys are, not you," Batman said, crossing his arms.

"I know who the bad guys are too," said Robin. "Not just you." And he kicked Batman in the shin and then danced out of Batman's reach.

Batman lunged at Robin, and I caught him by the cape.

"Cut it out," I said. I didn't want the janitor to hear us scuffling around. "You can get in a lot of trouble for fighting in school."

"Not if you're superheroes," said Robin.

"Yeah, superheroes are allowed to fight," agreed Batman.

They grinned at each other under their masks.

"Let's go," said Batman.

"Yeah," said Robin. "Let's go find some real crime."

"Wait," I said. It's not like I loved hanging out with these two, but I really needed the paint and paint-brushes, and it didn't look like I was going to get any help from Junchao. "Listen, a bad guy stole my paint and paintbrushes and put them in there, and I have to get them back. Won't you help me?"

My plea for help worked like a charm. My super-heroes were totally into me again. "Which bad guy is he? Is he the guy who broke your arm?" Batman asked.

"Um, he has a big belly and he jingles when he walks," I started.

"Santa Claus?" asked Robin in a sad voice.

"Not Santa Claus, Robin," said Batman. "The janitor."

"Ohhhh," breathed Robin.

I shook my head yes.

"We've been after him for years!" cried Batman. "Let's go. I bet we can get in through the pottery room." He took off running down the hall, turning for just a second to stick his tongue out at his partner in crime-fighting. "I told you I know more about this place than you do."

That got Robin moving. He chased after Batman, his yellow bath towel flapping behind him.

Why do little kids always have to run everywhere? These two looked around Sunny's age, but Sunny never ran—unless she was running from me! I thought about Sunny stuck up in the tree with one boot, and I smiled. *I hope she has tree branches digging into her bony butt right now.* Then I took off after my superheroes.

We crossed a tiny enclosed hallway over a gully with shrubs growing underneath it. This school was kind of interesting. We climbed up a back staircase and into a big room with giant round steel machines and tons of white bowls and stuff on shelves. Obviously, it was the pottery room. I kind of liked the way it smelled. As I scurried to keep up with the kids, I swiped a handful of white pottery dust from one of the wooden tables and smeared it on my T-shirt and jeans. Probably artists always had plaster or clay dust on them.

The Caped Crusaders opened a back door, and we were inside the art room. The locked door that we had first tried was across the room.

"So where's your stuff?" asked Batman.

"Yeah, where's your artist stuff?" repeated Robin.

"Stop repeating me," said Batman.

"I didn't repeat you exactly," said Robin.

"You did too," said Batman.

"Did not," said Robin.

A key clicked in the door. The three of us dashed behind a display case. The janitor swung open the door and pushed a rolling cart into the room. His keys jangled at his waist, and he whistled as he walked. I turned to Batman and Robin and held my finger to my lips to shush them. I followed it with a smile that said "Everything is okay" and "Isn't this fun" at the same time. Batman and Robin giggled silently, falling into each other. I forgot that their dad was the math teacher here. I knew exactly how they were feeling. Back at my old school, I could have hidden in any room I wanted. In fact, because my dad was the principal, I had been allowed to roam free throughout the entire school all the time. Sunny too. Mostly we hung out in the gym or in the auditorium.

Sunny and I used to play hide-and-seek in the auditorium, where we'd turn out all the lights. It was pitch black. You couldn't even see your hand right in front of your face. If you weren't "it," you'd have to listen for the other person knocking around the chairs and stay away from the sounds. If you were "it," you'd have to walk around quietly trying to hear the other person breathing. We would always end up with a ton of bruises on our shins from stumbling into the rows of chairs or the stage or from falling on the stairs. Sunny was such a creepy little thing in the dark. I used to freak out when I heard her getting close to me. It was the most fun in the world.

Hiding out behind a dusty display case in the art room when your dad isn't in charge of the school wasn't so much fun. This janitor was sure to recognize me from the window incident. He'd think I was sneaking around again, which I guess I was. I signaled the giggly masked heroes to stay quiet. The janitor was still bumping around by the door. I wanted to peek out and check on him. We were pretty far from the back door to the pottery room. I motioned for the boys to stay put. Their eyes glowed back at me through their masks. I put my finger back to my lips and opened up my eyes wide to make sure they understood to be quiet, and then I crawled over to the edge of the display case.

When I got to the end of the case I saw them— paintbrushes, lots of them. I silently pulled a bunch of the brushes from the shelf. I looked behind me to Batman and Robin with an "Aha, I found my stuff!" face, and then I slipped them into my pocket.

QUACK . . . QUACK, QUACK, QUACK.

The three of us stared at one another with our mouths hanging open. I was so shocked that I didn't even shut my phone off, and the second ring sounded even louder than the first.

QUACK . . . QUACK, QUACK, QUACK.

"What the—" I heard the janitor say.

On the third ring—QUACK . . . QUACK, QUACK, QUACK—Batman and Robin flew out from behind the display case, jumping into the air and landing in front of the janitor with their capes flapping and their hands on their hips.

"We have you now!" shouted Batman.

"Hey," growled the janitor, "what are you two doing in here?" He didn't react to the costumes at all. He obviously knew exactly who these two masked boys were.

QUACK . . . QUACK, QUACK—the fourth and final ring was muffled by the squawk of a radio, followed by a booming woman's voice, "Jim, Jim. Where are you?"

"Gosh darn it," the janitor said. He picked up his radio. "What is it?"

I stayed crouched behind the display case while the Dark Knight and Boy Wonder remained in their superhero stance, challenging the janitor who was no longer paying any attention to them.

"We need the storeroom door opened up in the

kitchen, and I don't have the key," crackled a voice from the radio.

"I'll be down in a second," sighed the janitor. "And you don't have to shout into that thing. I keep telling you that over and over again," he muttered. "You boys stop the fooling around and get back downstairs," he said.

"We don't listen to bad guys," said Batman.

"Yeah, we don't listen to bad guys," repeated Robin.

I peeked through the shelving and watched the janitor shaking his head while he pushed his cart out of the room. There was moment of silence, and then we heard the door shut with a soft *poof.*

Batman and Robin let out one solid scream and high-fived each other. Robin smiled over at me, and I noticed he was missing one of his front teeth. "That was so fun. What are we gonna do next?"

These two were ready for another adventure while I was still shaking from almost getting caught. Back at my old school, I wasn't scared of the janitors. Joe and Sid were our friends, and they loved Sunny and me. They let us use the giant broom to help clean the school. The broom took up the entire hallway. Mostly Sunny and I just used it to play tag. It was so fun to race down the hall after each other. You couldn't get away from it because it took up every inch of the hallway from wall to wall.

There was a row of old paint cans storing stuff like rags and sponges and more paintbrushes. I plucked one filled with rags from the shelf and dumped out the rags. The color on the can was blue, not red—but who cares, it was just a prop. I wanted to be gone from here.

QUACK . . . QUACK, QUACK, QUACK.

The two boys leaped in the air.

QUACK . . . QUACK, QUACK, QUACK.

I looked down at my phone. *Sunny.*

I clicked my phone on.

"Stay in your tree," I spit and then switched it off.

Batman and Robin bounced up into my face. "Who's in a tree? Who's in a tree? Who's in a tree?"

"I have to go," I said.

They leaped after me, yipping and yapping like two excited puppies, begging me not to leave them.

"Okay, okay, you can come with me. Just be quiet," I told them. I didn't need the janitor coming back and asking about my "normal" props.

They immediately obeyed and were silent, although Robin kept bouncing up and down. Batman pulled something out of his pocket. "Kneel down," he said.

I thought, *I am about to be knighted.*

He leaned over and drew a big *P* on my T-shirt. Great, like I needed one more thing to add to the dust and the paint and the cast and my bald head.

"You're Paintgirl now," he said, his breath smelling a little like Cheez Doodles. But I have to admit, the way they stared so seriously out of their masks at me made my heart glow. *I am Paintgirl.*

"Do you want me to draw a mask on your face with my marker?" Batman asked.

"No." I giggled. "The *P* is good."

Maybe this whole weird behavior thing was coming a little too easily to me.

It's a Bird, It's a Plane, It's Paintgirl

We walked back down the staircase and over the bridge. "Is there a back door that I can get out of? You know, so that the janitor doesn't get me."

Batman and Robin looked at each other.

"Maybe the one by the gym?" suggested Robin, sticking his finger in the hole where his tooth once was.

"No, the science fair's in the gym," I said. Even with my "normal" props, I wasn't in the mood to pass through a crowd.

"I know," said Batman. "How about the back

door that leads to the soccer field?" The words had no sooner left his mouth than his cape was flapping behind him as he raced away from us.

"He thinks that because he's Batman he knows everything," Robin grumbled.

I nodded. I also had a know-it-all in my life. And then the two of us took off after the flapping black cape.

As Batman approached the end of the hall he slowed and started tiptoeing. Robin and I slowed and started tiptoeing too. Batman stopped and peeked around the corner to check it out. And then he snapped his head back, throwing himself up against the hallway wall. Robin and I smashed up against the wall too, and my paint can whacked into the cement. The two of them narrowed their eyes at the racket I made. I mouthed, "I'm sorry." But then Batman giggled and danced around the corner. He had just been fooling with us. Robin and I exchanged an annoyed look and then followed him.

He headed toward a door at the end of the hallway. We were about twenty feet behind him. As he

ran past an open office door, we heard someone shout,
"What are you doing out there, Stanley?"

Robin and I froze.

Batman skipped back to the office door and jumped
around in place. "Hi, Mrs. Hull. I'm running around,"
he answered honestly.

"Well, stop before you get hurt," said the voice. "You should be in the gym at the fair with your father."

"I don't have a father. He got killed by bad guys," Batman said.

"Yes, I remember now. Well, Batman, you still need to go back to the gym. I'm sure you're not supposed to be running around by yourself."

Batman looked down the hall at us with a frown, not knowing what to do.

I motioned for him to come back toward us.

"Okay," he said to the voice, walking away.

And then the three of us tiptoed farther down the hallway and squished into a doorway together.

"Now what do we do?" asked Robin.

"Do you know another way out?" I asked Batman.

He rolled his eyes up into his mask and thought. "The only other way is back past the science fair."

All three of us slumped a bit against the door.

"I have an idea," said Batman. "We'll go out past that one gym door by the water fountains and the trophy cases. That door is far away from the stage. Maybe there won't be so many people by it. We can run and slide by the doors on our knees so nobody sees us. I'll go first, and then you and Paintgirl can go."

"Why can't I go first?" asked Robin. "Why do you get to go first?"

"Wait a minute," I said, standing up a little straighter. "Mrs. Hull doesn't know me. I can walk right out of here and start for home this very minute." I looked down the hall past Mrs. Hull's office at the double doors leading out to the soccer field, stunned by this great idea.

"But those aren't your paintbrushes, and that isn't your paint can either," said Batman. "And we'll tell Mrs. Hull on you if you don't keep playing."

Wow. Robin was right, Batman was a know-it-all.

"Um," I said. "Okay, let's do the sliding thing."

We peeked out from the doorway and looked both ways, and then Batman led us toward the water fountains and the trophy case. From the sound of the crowd, I could tell we were getting closer to the science fair. I swung my paint can in one hand and held onto my brushes with my cast hand. All I cared about was hiding from the janitor. Now that I looked like an artist, real people could see me because I was officially normal now, although I was still on some strange secret mission with a couple of masked crusaders.

My phone buzzed with a text. It was Sunny again.

Where are you?

Coming, I texted back. And then I smiled. Wait until she saw me . . . normal, calm, artist me.

The crowd noises were getting louder. I held the paintbrushes out in front of me and swung the can of paint in a bigger arc. My stomach gave a nervous gurgle. *Be normal*, I commanded.

Batman approached the doors and looked in. And then he backed up two feet and threw his fist in the air. "I am the night!" he proclaimed, hopping twice and sliding down the hall past the open gym doors. Once on the other side, he stood up, adjusted his cape, and brushed the hallway dust from his jeans.

"Yeah!" whispered Robin.

Batman peeked into the gym doorway again and then he waved to his partner. Robin took off running and slid across the doorway. There was not a single break in the murmuring of the crowd. No one noticed

either masked munchkin sliding by the open door. But why would they? They were all busy at the fair, plus it seemed like all the people in this school knew Batman and Robin.

The two of them motioned me on. I rolled my eyes at them. They motioned bigger. *I can't believe I allowed myself to be roped into this. Oh well. Am I Paintgirl or not?* I decided I was.

I held my paint can up in the air and banged my paintbrushes on it three times. This seemed like a good Paintgirl gesture. Then I took a running start and bent my knees to slide down the hall past the open doors to the gym. My heart gave a little jump with excitement. This was kind of fun.

Just as I crouched into my slide, I caught sight of a familiar head right inside the fair doors, or rather a familiar "white" head. . . . It was the boy with the perfect signature on my cast, Michael Capezzi. And he still wore the cast on his head from the surgery to take out a brain tumor.

The last thing I wanted was Michael Capezzi seeing me covered in red splotches! I tried to stop midslide, but my sneaker caught on the floor and I tumbled, paint-can-over-head and head-over-paint-can. My paint-brushes went flying. I landed at the feet of the stunned superheroes and crawled like a crazy crab down the hall and away from the doors of the gym. I was in such a hurry to get out of sight that I didn't watch where I was scuttling and ended up crashing into two legs. I heard the jingling of keys and knew what I'd done.

The janitor looked down at me. His eyes narrowed with suspicion as he took in the red splotches and pottery dust. I couldn't help imagining all the wrong things he was imagining I'd done, and I squirmed on the floor.

"What's going on here?" he boomed.

"She's Paintgirl," said Batman.

"I'm a good guy," I choked as I scrambled to gather my paintbrushes and can.

"Boys." His voice was soft and kind. "Your dad has been looking for you two. You better head back into the gymnasium now."

"But . . . ," Batman started, looking up at me for help.

"And you," he muttered. "Are you part of the fair?"

"Um, no," I said.

"Then you don't belong here," he said, glaring down at me.

"Okay," I said, getting off the floor.

"Where are your parents?"

"My sister's waiting for me out by the parking lot," I said. I didn't mention that she was six years old and up in a tree.

"Get going, then," he said. And then to himself he muttered, "I don't have time for this today."

I started down the hall toward the door. I could feel his eyes watching to make sure I actually left the school. I kept my head down and walked while I listened to the loud complaints of my fellow superheroes trying to convince the janitor to let them follow me. The janitor's words *you don't belong here* rang in my head like an unanswered phone. It was like Sunny's ketchup had turned me into a bad kid. And maybe the dust helped, and the giant black *P* on my chest . . . But still . . . it was all just stuff *on* me, not stuff *in* me.

I pushed open the door of the school and was hit with a cool breeze of outside air. It felt so good to be back out. It only took me two turns around the brick building to put me back under Sunny Sweet's tree.

"Masha!"

Sunny's eyes were wide with fear. She looked totally freaked out. For one split second I felt sorry for her up there. I guess I had been in the school a long time. But then I remembered how mean the janitor had just been to me and that Michael Capezzi had almost seen me sprawled out in a hallway splattered with red junk and pottery dust! I put a fake smile on my face while I hugged my paint can and paintbrushes to my chest. We were a simple bus ride away from home, and I intended to act normal the entire way.

"Why are you still up in that tree, sister dear?" I asked pleasantly.

"You told me to stay here," she said.

"Come down from there before you get hurt," I commanded in a voice dripping with love and concern.

"Masha?" Sunny's eyes got even wider.

The Simple Bus Ride

Are you okay, Masha?" Sunny asked, clomping alongside me with her one rain boot.

"Absolutely, sister dearest," I drawled. "I'm just happy to be heading home."

"Why are you carrying that can of paint and those brushes?"

A man and a lady walked toward us as we made our way to the bus stop. Mom and I had looked up the bus map last night, and the bus stop was only three blocks away. The lady carried a baby strapped to her chest. The baby faced us, and its arms and legs stuck out into the air like it was skydiving off its mom. I saw the man and lady take one look at me, then turn and look at each other, and then look back at me.

"I'm an artist," I said cheerily, as Sunny and I reached them.

They both gave me these big phony smiles, and the man reached up and held the lady's arm as Sunny and I walked past them.

"You're an artist?" asked Sunny, hopping in front of me.

I walked around her and continued to head toward the bus stop while swinging my paint can a little more.

"That's so cool, Masha! Can I be one too?" she asked.

I fought the urge to bop her in the head with my can. She wasn't supposed to believe me! She was supposed to be in awe of how I turned things around on her.

"I'm not really an artist," I said.

"But you just said . . ."

"Sunny, forget it," I snapped. "Anyway, aren't you

even a little bit upset that we're going home and not staying for the fair?" I asked.

"Um," she said, adjusting the rain hat on her head. "My hypothesis wasn't connected to a particular environment."

"What?" I said. "Never mind, let's just get to the bus, Sunny." All I wanted right now was to be home, home, home.

"What's that *P* for on your shirt?" she asked.

"It's nothing," I said. "And take off that dumb hat, will you?"

She looked at me out of the corner of her eye and pulled the hat down firmly over her ears. I just shook my head and kept walking.

We got to the bus stop without passing anybody else. The bench was empty except for someone's leftover McDonald's lunch sitting in the middle. There was also a horrible pile of dog poop next to the bus stop sign. There were flies everywhere.

We stood off to the side, away from the flies. I stared down the road, searching for a sight of the bus. Sunny stared at the flies.

"They're laying eggs in the dog poop."

"Don't tell me those things," I said.

"Imagine being born in dog poop," she added.

"Sunny, stop! Where is the bus?" I checked the bus app on my phone.

"They might lay them in the hamburger too," Sunny said. "I'd rather be born in a half-eaten hamburger. What about you?"

The app said bus number 55, our bus, would be here in eleven minutes. It was going to be a long eleven minutes.

"Masha," Sunny said, grabbing my arm. "Give me your paint can and one of your brushes. I want to grab some of the dog poop to take home."

"What? No stinkin' way!" I said, holding it out of her reach.

"Please, please, please, please," she said, jumping for the can. "I wanna see the flies hatch."

I spotted the bus coming. That was not eleven minutes, thank goodness!

We fought over the can while the bus pulled up and opened its doors. I jumped on. Sunny didn't.

"Get on this bus," I said.

"No." She stomped her rain-booted foot.

"This isn't playtime," the bus driver muttered, looking at me and then raising his eyebrows.

I growled at my sister. "You cannot bring dog poop onto the bus."

"Okay, off the bus," the driver said.

I turned to him. "Wait one second; she's going to get on."

The bus driver sighed, wiping his face with his hands. Then he glanced down at Sunny. "Are you two alone?"

I thought it best to ignore that question. I could tell he just wanted to drive his bus.

"Sunny, get on the . . ." I could see that she had me, mostly because she could see that she had me. I wanted her to get on the bus, and she wanted the fly eggs. I held out the can. "The hamburger, not the dog poop! And be careful not to step on anything with your sock."

She cracked a smile bigger than a circus clown and grabbed the can and ran to the bench. The bus driver tried to close the doors, but I stood in between them.

"Please, we're getting on," I begged.

Sunny leaped into me and onto the bus. The driver slammed the doors shut. We walked toward the back through a sea of staring eyes. Of course Sunny didn't notice a thing. She was too busy grinning at her fly eggs.

We sat about two-thirds from the back of the bus in the first two empty seats I found together. I hunched down and half closed my eyes, trying to pretend that no one was looking at us. Be normal . . . Wasn't that what Alice said? Okay . . . normal. I opened my eyes and sat up straight in my seat, trying to look like a model bus rider. It was hard with Sunny sitting next to me poking at her half-eaten hamburger with the end of one of my paintbrushes.

"What's in the can?" asked a little kid sitting in front of us. "Is it alive?"

"Turn around, Jeremy," his mother said. Jeremy didn't listen.

"It's a hamburger," Sunny said. "The meat is no longer alive, but there is something alive inside the meat."

The little kid began to drool. "A dinosaur?" he asked.

"Dinosaurs have been extinct for sixty-five million years," Sunny answered. "There are fly eggs in this hamburger. Want to see them?"

"No," I said.

"Fly eggs!" said the kid. He got up on his knees and leaned over. Again his mother told him to turn around. Again the kid didn't listen. I sat up even straighter and folded my hands together on my lap, trying so hard to look normal.

"Wow," the kid breathed in my face. "How did the fly eggs get in there?"

"The flies laid the eggs in there."

"Are they gonna hatch and fly out on the bus?"

I glanced around the bus to see if anybody heard that. I hoped that this wasn't going to happen. The bus driver would *really* throw us off then.

"No, no," said Sunny. "When the eggs hatch, they'll be larvae, or what we call maggots . . ."

"Okay," I said, interrupting. "Maggots" had gotten everyone's attention on the bus. Jeremy's mother turned around and pulled him down into the seat. She caught sight of me, and I saw her frown. I tried to brush some of the pottery dust off me, but it seemed to be totally stuck to my T-shirt.

Sunny went back to playing with her hamburger.

"I think I see the eggs under the pickle."

"Stop poking at them," I whispered. She didn't stop.

I looked out the window so I didn't have to watch her hunt for fly eggs in a gross blob of mustard. We were passing a seafood restaurant that Sunny, Mom, Mrs. Song, and I had eaten in once. I didn't remember it being anywhere near our house. A tiny sick feeling wiggled in my stomach, and it had nothing to do with maggots. The bus took a left at the light and headed in what felt like another wrong direction. I looked around at the faces on the bus like someone might look familiar—or maybe something about them would clue me in to where we were heading. I wanted to lean forward and ask Jeremy's mom where we were, but after her frown I couldn't bring myself to do it.

I clicked on my phone and brought up the bus map. The 55's route was a red line winding its way around the city and passing a few blocks away from our house. I looked back out the window at the unfamiliar houses and stores and then over at Sunny. She was totally focused on her fly eggs. I tried to think if I'd looked at the number on the front of the bus when it pulled up. Lots of buses used the same bus stop, and you had to make sure you got on the one with the right number. I was sure that I remembered seeing that big white 55 lit up over the top of the windshield. But I knew that I hadn't. I was too busy trying to keep Sunny from scooping up dog poop.

Maybe I should go ask the driver. But then I'd have to stand up and walk through the bus, and it wasn't like he loved us. And he might even ask about our parents again. I was starting to sweat. I couldn't stand it anymore. I leaned forward to ask Jeremy's mother just as her phone rang. I sat back. That's when I realized I needed to use the bathroom. Ugh.

Jeremy turned around. "Let me see the maggots," he whispered.

His mother was busy talking on the phone and didn't notice he'd turned around again. I wished she would. I didn't need this kid's face in mine right now.

"Sunny," I said.

"Hmm," she answered, not listening.

I couldn't stop myself and tapped Jeremy's mom on the shoulder. "What bus is this?" I asked in my sweetest voice ever.

"One minute," Jeremy's mother said into her phone in an annoyed voice. She glanced back over the bus seat at me, taking in all of my splotchiness and giving me another disapproving frown. It's like Sunny had turned me into some kind of monster. And all it took was a single bottle of ketchup! "The 57," she said, and then she returned to her phone conversation.

"Thanks," I croaked, sitting back. My eyes stung and a cold wind swirled through my chest. How did I get us on the wrong bus? But I knew how.

"Why are you dirty?" asked Jeremy. "And why does she only have one boot on?"

I ignored him. "Sunny." I nudged her. "Sunny, we're on the wrong bus."

She looked up calmly from her can, the brim of her hat sitting on top of her blond eyebrows. "Let me check what time it is," she said.

"What does it matter what time it is?" I asked.

"No reason," she said.

"What do you mean, *no reason*?" Sunny never did anything without a reason.

She blinked at me. And then she reminded me that we were lost. "How about we get off this bus and get on one that takes us home?"

I glanced out the window. We were passing old broken-down highways and piles of sand and gravel. "We can't get out here," I said. "I have to go to the bathroom."

"Number one or number two?" asked Jeremy.

"What?"

"Do you have to go number one or number two?" he repeated.

"He's asking if you have to—" Sunny broke in.

"I know what he's asking," I said. Then I turned so I faced Sunny only, trying to give Jeremy the hint that this was a private conversation. "I'll ring the bell to get off as soon as I see a restaurant or a gas station or something. Be ready to get off."

"Can I have a fly egg to take home?" Jeremy asked.

"I need them for an experiment that I'm doing," Sunny told him.

"You can't do an experiment, you're a little kid."

Sunny paid no attention. "I'm thinking I might do something related to forensic entomology, you know, the study of insects and other arthropods. I've done some work on mass temperature. It's kind of interesting because sometimes this data can be used to tell how long a human body has been dead. The mass temperature of the gathering of maggots in a dead body can give a pretty accurate time of death."

"You're weird," Jeremy said.

"No, she's not," I shot back at him. Although I had to admit the dead body thing freaked me out a little too.

He stuck his tongue out at us and turned around.

I looked at Sunny. She shrugged, like she had no idea where that came from. Well, it wasn't all bad because the kid was pretty annoying. I seemed to be scaring off the adults, and Sunny was taking care of the kids. We were like a freaky Dynamic Duo.

The flash of a big blue coffee cup sign caught my eye. It was The Mug, and that meant a bathroom! I quickly pressed the yellow strip to stop the bus. Within five seconds, the bus pulled over and I dragged Sunny and her fly eggs off. I could feel everybody on the bus sigh—*Thank goodness those kids are gone.* The driver slammed the doors shut behind us.

"Hurry," I said to Sunny, running for the coffee shop. "I really have to go!"

Sunny ran behind me, holding out her hamburger/fly egg combo-in-a-can. Her booted foot scraped the road with each step, followed by the silence of her sock—scrape, silence, scrape, silence, scrape, silence. "Did you know that your bladder is a muscle and right now you're exercising it?" she called at my back.

"Stop talking," I yelled.

"It can hold up to two full cups of pee-pee. So probably right now your bladder has about that much in it," she continued.

"Sunny!" I shouted. My little sister understands how the universe was made but not how wrong it is to talk about someone else's pee-pee. Or that you don't call it pee-pee!

You Say Pariah,
I Say Piranha

Sunny took a big bite out of her sausage-and-egg sandwich. Then she studied the hamburger in the can at our table in The Mug.

"Put that thing on the floor."

"No, someone might kick it over."

That was true. And a disgusting half-eaten hamburger all over the floor was probably worse than a disgusting half-eaten hamburger sitting in a can. Plus I knew that this wouldn't end the stinky burger story, or I'd kick it over myself. Sunny would just stick the gross thing back in the can. I shuddered when I thought about touching that fly-filled piece of meat.

Two teenagers walked over to the table next to us, took one look at me, and then without even speaking chose another table on the other side of the dining room. It was like they had used telepathy to decide not to sit anywhere near me.

"You made me a piranha," I moaned.

"A piranha is a fish with very sharp teeth that eats meat," she said. "I'm an excellent scientist, but not good enough to turn you into a freshwater fish."

"Yet," I said.

"What you mean is that I turned you into a pariah," she said. "A pariah is an outcast, someone who doesn't fit in with everybody else."

How does she know what I meant? But the fact that she actually did know what I meant made my head feel like it was going to pop right off my body. "Yeah, well, maybe I did mean piranha. Maybe I do feel like you made me into a meat-eating fish."

She pushed her gross hamburger bucket toward me. "Want some lunch, fishy-fishy?" she asked, giggling.

"Cut it out," I said.

Sunny put down her sausage-and-egg sandwich and pulled out her notebook.

"Sunny," I groaned.

"So, you feel like a fish," she said, scribbling away, "out of water?"

"Just eat your hamburger—I mean your egg sandwich—and leave me alone. And why are you still wearing Mom's stupid rain hat? Take it off." I picked up my phone and started checking out the map to see how the heck I was going to get us home.

Sunny ate her sandwich and scribbled in her notebook while carefully studying her fly eggs. But I knew perfectly well that she was writing about me.

A text came in from Alice.

Are you home yet?

I sighed and tapped "Alice" in my favorites. There was no way to text what we'd just been through. I had to call.

"No!" I said into the phone.

"Where are you?"

"At The Mug on . . ." I switched over to my map. "Washington Avenue and Thornton Street."

"Why?"

"Oh, Alice, I got us on the wrong bus."

There was silence for a minute. And then Alice burst out, "Masha! You're right across Fairlawn Cemetery from the hospital!"

"So?"

"So? Come here."

"No way, Alice!" I shouted, making everyone in the coffee shop turn just a little more away from Sunny and me than they already were. "No way. No way," I said more quietly. "I need to get *home*."

"Did you find the paint can and the paintbrushes?"

"Yes."

"Then you look normal. Why can't you just walk across the cemetery and say hi?"

I breathed in deeply through my nose and looked at Sunny in her stupid rain hat and single boot. I didn't have the heart to tell Alice that the paint can and brushes weren't exactly working. No one believed the artist thing. They were seeing Sunny's idea of me— they were seeing me as different. "I can't walk into that hospital, Alice. It's been less than two weeks since I stole a cast and ran out of there."

"Okay, you don't have to come in. I'll meet you out front. And you can catch the 68 home. You know the bus. It's the exact same one you took home last time. Anyway, what bus would you take from The Mug on Washington? The 68 might just be the closest bus to you right now. I bet it's the fastest way for you to get home."

Shoot . . . She was making sense. I could hear her ticking away on her keyboard. "It looks like you can walk here straight through the graveyard."

"Through a graveyard? There has to be a faster way home."

"There's not. And it's not even a mile."

"A mile?"

"Did you know that some people can run a mile in less than four minutes?" Alice said.

"Those people aren't dragging their little sisters around," I told her.

The thought of walking a mile through a graveyard wasn't sounding so good, but the only other idea I could think of at the moment was to call my mom. I actually considered it for about a second. But then I pictured her pulling up to The Mug with a disappointed face because I couldn't manage a simple science fair. And on top of this, I'd have to explain Sunny's missing boot and her bucket of maggots. I just knew I couldn't do it. Instead, I imagined my mom sitting in her painting class, leaning her face up close to her canvas. She always leaned up close to her painting when she was working. For some reason, she looked really pretty when she did that. Maybe concentrating on something hard made you pretty. I glanced over at Sunny staring down intently into her maggot bucket. Maybe it depended on what you were concentrating on.

"Masha? Are you still there?"

"Okay," I said. "We'll come."

Alice screeched with happiness. "Text me when you're almost here, and I'll come downstairs and meet you outside."

"How will you get out?"

"Don't worry about that, just get over here." She giggled. "And Masha?"

"Yeah?"

"Thanks," she said.

"I'd do anything for you," I told her. And it was true. I would. "You're my best friend."

There was a tiny bit of silence.

"I never had a best friend before," she whispered.

Me neither, I thought. I wondered if it was weird to make it all the way until the fifth grade and never have had a best friend. Back at my old home in Pennsylvania, I'd played with lots of different kids. And at my new school I had been hanging out with Junchao a lot. But I hadn't ever been super close to one person. It seemed that in books or movies there were best friends popping up all over the place—kids had them, adults had them, even dogs and cats and robots had them. But in real life, they didn't just get passed out like cake at a birthday party.

"And so now you do," I told her. "And your best friend is about to walk through some creepy graveyard covered in paint and pottery dust, dragging her little sister, who is wearing one boot and carrying a pail of larvae."

"Lar-*vee*, not lar-*vah*," corrected Sunny without taking her eyes from her can.

"What?" asked Alice.

"Never mind," I told her. "I'll be there as soon as I can."

I hung up and smiled at my phone. I wasn't a fish or an outcast. I was Alice Rottersdam's best friend.

The Informal Diagonal Line Game

Let's go," I said.

"Wait. I have to . . . do something," Sunny said.

"What?"

"Um." I could tell she was thinking something up.

"You don't have to do anything, Sunny."

"Yes, I do," she said. "I have to go to the bathroom."

"Right."

"I do. Here," she said, leaning her stomach toward me. "You want to push on my bladder? It's full."

"No, I don't want to touch your bladder," I said, moving away from her.

She threw her head back and laughed from deep within her skinny little neck. All her tiny teeth were on display, like a yawning shark.

"It's not funny. Listen, you can't go in there with just a sock on your foot. Here," I said, taking off my sneaker. "Just put it on and tie the laces tight." My foot felt weirdly cold not having a shoe on it in the middle of a coffee shop.

Sunny put on my sneaker and placed my mom's rain hat neatly on the table. It was the first time she'd taken it off today. Then she glanced up at the clock on the wall.

"Why do you keep checking the time?" I asked.

"Watch my fly eggs," she said.

"Are they going to hatch?"

"Not for a few hours at least," she said. "I just don't want anybody to take them."

"Oh yeah," I said. "They are definitely in danger of being stolen."

As soon as Sunny walked away and I was by myself at the table, I felt blotchier and dustier. It was as if I became even more different without Sunny next to me. I stared down at the crumbs on the tabletop and tried to think normal thoughts, but I still felt like I stuck out. I tapped my paintbrushes on Sunny's empty plate to make them more noticeable and pulled the can of paint a little closer to me. But the smell of the old meat hit me in the nose, and I had to push it away.

Sunny came back with a fistful of mustard packets and stuck the rain hat back on.

"I knew it. I knew you didn't have to use the bathroom. What are you doing?"

"My eggs will dry out," she whined. "You have to keep them moist so they hatch. If we're going to be taking a long walk in the sun, they might die."

She squirted the mustard onto the hamburger. "Oh gross, Sunny." I couldn't take much more of this. I could see the people around us grimacing as they watched out of the corners of their eyes. And they had no idea what was in that bucket!

"Let's go." I stood up and scrunched my jeans

down a bit so they would fall over my shoeless foot. I'd just let Sunny keep my sneaker. I walked out of the coffee shop. Sunny followed, staring into her bucket and bumping into me every other second. "Get your eyes off those eggs and watch where you're going." We walked down the little sidewalk that led us toward the back of the building. I stopped to look both ways before we crossed the parking lot and Sunny rammed into my back. "Do that again and I'm going to dump you in the graveyard," I snapped.

She didn't even react. Her calm face made me want to drop to the ground screaming and frothing at the mouth. She always seemed to be able to make me the most mad when she did nothing!

I turned and started walking across the parking lot toward the archway. It said FAIRLAWN CEMETERY at the top of the gate in curly, black letters. I took long, fast strides, not caring whether or not Sunny kept up. The parking lot felt warm through my sock. I could hear Sunny scraping behind me in her one boot, with the scrape now followed by the clomp of my sneaker on her other foot.

I had only been inside a big graveyard like this once. It was back when I was about eight and Sunny was still in a stroller. My mom and dad took us to Gettysburg, where there had been a big battle during

the Civil War. I don't remember that much about it, but just that my dad and mom held hands during the movie we watched before we walked in the graveyard across the street from the park's center. It was cozy and dark in the theater, and I leaned against my dad's arm. I can still smell the warm cotton of his shirt. I totally belonged in that place and that time. The thing is, when you belong, you don't know that you belong. You only know that you once belonged when you don't belong anymore. Standing outside the archway of the Fairlawn Cemetery, I didn't feel like I belonged at all. The janitor's face popped into my head, along with his words *you don't belong here.* I snapped at my little sister to get him out of my mind. "Hurry up, Sunny."

We walked into the graveyard and started down one of the little roads.

"Wait!" Sunny called. "Shouldn't we take one of those maps with us?" She pointed at a little shedlike structure that said INFORMATION on it. On the outside of the shed there were a few rows of wooden shelves containing maps.

"No," I said, even though I stinkin' knew that this was a mistake. I just didn't want her to be right . . . again. A person can get pretty tired of her six-year-old little sister always knowing more than her. "We're going to walk straight across the graveyard to the hospital."

"But the roads look like they go in loops," she said, looking up ahead of us.

"I said we don't need it. We're not going to take the roads. We're going to walk straight across the grass."

"On people's graves?" she asked.

"They're dead, Sunny. They won't care."

She glanced one last time at the rack of maps and then back at me. But she didn't move.

"You can carry around a gross pail of lar-*veee*, but you're all freaked out about walking over a few graves?"

I turned back and walked out onto the graves. I was completely freaked out, but I pretended that I was simply walking in a park and not over the top of dead people. I really wished I had both sneakers on, though. The grass felt so spongy. "Come on," I said. "It will be like a game. We have to walk in a diagonal line through the graveyard to the gate across from the hospital, no matter what. We can call it the Diagonal Line Game."

"Is the cemetery in the shape of a polygon?"

"I don't know," I said.

"Well, if it isn't a polygon then we can't walk a formal diagonal line because a diagonal line is a line joining two points of a polygon."

I stopped walking and turned around. "I'm going to poly-*gong* you right on your head," I told her.

She thought for a second and then said, "I know, Masha, we can walk an *informal* diagonal line. Informally, any sloping line can be called diagonal."

"Okay, Sunny, let's just keep walking. All I want is to be home right now."

She shook her head yes, the giant rain hat bobbing up and down on her head. I turned and started back over the graves.

"Masha," she said, following behind me. "Can we can call it the Informal Diagonal Line Game? You know, so it's named correctly?"

"Sunny Sweet, we are in the middle of a graveyard, and if you don't be quiet, I'm going to start digging your grave right this minute."

"Okay, Masha, no problem," she said. "We can call the game your name. I mean, lots of things are misnamed. Did you know that the word 'alligator' is a misspelling of the Spanish words 'el lagarto' for 'the lizard'? And take the *Bufo marinus* toad. That toad can live just about anywhere *except* in a marine environment!" She snorted. "Get it? A *marinus* toad that can't swim."

"Sunny," I growled. "Alice is waiting for us. So stop talking and start walking."

We trudged off across the graves. I was careful not to step directly on the gravestones that were laid flat in the grass. Weirdly, the graveyard was kind of a pretty place. The headstones were all different sizes. Some were very pointy and high, like the Washington Monument, and others were like little houses with doors and tiny front lawns surrounded by miniature iron fences. The grass was bright green, like it had been fed a ton of lawn food. And there were flowers and colorful wreaths in front of many of the gravestones. Even the trees were pretty. They all looked like trees out of a little kid's drawing. They had solid, straight trunks with a rounded top of leaves like a perfect piece of broccoli. But the best part about this place was that being covered in red splotches and pottery dust was no big deal to dead people. I could forget about Sunny's crazy experiment and just think about how I would get to say hi to Alice, and then we'd be home, home, home . . . and eating Mrs. Song's lip-smacking dumplings, and this whole day would soon be washed off in a really, really long shower.

Sunny walked beside me, swinging her bucket and humming. I tried not to think about the eggs in the hamburger, but then I couldn't get them out of my head. "So, Sunny, how do flies lay their eggs in dead bodies if they're buried in the ground?"

"They don't," she chirped. "It used to be that scientists thought that things could come alive out of dead stuff like hamburgers or dog poop. They called it spontaneous generation. They even thought that mice could grow out of dirty underwear mixed with wheat."

"No way," I said.

"Yes way." She giggled. "Of course live things can't pop out of dirty underwear, except for maybe Freddie Winniger's underwear."

We laughed. Freddie Winniger was this kid in Sunny's class who was always teasing her. He called her silly names like Stormy and Rainy. But he also called her The Freak. Back in our old school, because my dad was principal, everybody knew Sunny and nobody teased her. She was even allowed to hang out in Dad's office when she got bored in class. In our new school, she was stuck in the classroom with Freddie. Once when I saw Freddie burp in Sunny's face on her way out of school, I ran over and told him that he had better leave Sunny alone. He shouted that he didn't have to listen to me. I remember Sunny nodding her head and saying, "He's right." I wanted to bop her in the head. I knew he was right, but maybe *he* didn't know he was right . . . and that was the whole point. Later, when Sunny wasn't watching, I found Freddie on the playground and told him that I was really a ghost and that if he didn't leave Sunny alone I was going to show up one night in his room and pull him under the bed and eat him. He called me a liar, but I could tell that he was spooked. Every time I saw him in the halls I tried to look like I was floating. He left Sunny alone after that.

"So if the flies can't lay their eggs in a buried body, how do maggots get into dead bodies?" I asked.

"I guess a fly can lay eggs in your dead body if you die and nobody finds you right away. But if you die and they bury you immediately, flies don't get to you. Instead, there are a lot of other things under there that will munch on you."

"Ugh, Sunny, don't tell me any more."

"Anyway," she continued, "it's mostly tiny little things called bacteria that eat you after you're dead, and then some insects that are already down there, like beetles and stuff."

"Okay, that's enough." I couldn't stand the thought of a thousand beetles chewing on me.

We headed up a small hill past another group of gravestones. They looked a lot like the last group we passed by. I read the names on the stones. They even sounded like the names on the last stones. As I looked around, all of a sudden the pretty green grass and

perfect trees all seemed a little too pretty and green and a little too perfect. I walked faster up to the top of the hill.

Once we got to the top, I thought for sure we'd at

least see the hospital, or maybe hear cars or something. But it was quiet, and all I saw were more creepy trees. "Let me borrow those binoculars, Sunny."

"What binoculars?"

"The ones you were spying on me with back at the school."

"Whoops, I left them in the tree."

Great. I started off down the hill toward a little forest of trees because I could see another tiny hill up ahead. I was really hoping that from the top of *that* hill we'd see the hospital.

"This is not diagonal," Sunny said.

"Yes, it is," I told her.

"No, it's not."

"Okay, it's not," I snapped.

"Do you know where we are?"

"Yes."

"No, you don't," she said.

"Yes, I do," I told her.

"No, you don't."

"Okay, I don't," I said. "But just come on. Maybe we'll see the hospital at the top of the next hill."

But we didn't.

Sunny stared at me. I hated when I could see so much of the white in her eyes.

"I know. I'll just use the map on my phone." I turned on the GPS. We immediately popped up as a tiny blue dot in the middle of a large, strangely shaped patch of green on the map—the cemetery. And even though we had passed over tiny roads with names like "Fir Avenue," "Snowdrop Place," and "Magnolia Street," none of these tiny roads were showing up in the green patch on my map.

"We should have taken a map from the front gate," Sunny said.

"We're fine," I said, although I wasn't so sure.

"Should we call Mommy?"

"No, Sunny. Just let me think."

Even though I would do just about anything to be home right now, I didn't want to call my mom. I wanted her to be able to finish her painting class, and I guess I wanted her to know that I could do this . . . take care of Sunny and myself. But could I? The sun was hot, and my T-shirt was sticking to my back.

When I thought about being here when the sun started to go down, tiny belly butterflies zoomed around in my stomach.

"I know!" I shouted, a little too loud. "All we have to do is start walking and watch the blue dot move on the map. I can see the hospital and I can see us, I just don't know which way to walk. Come on."

I started down the hill and under a bunch of perfect broccoli trees, keeping my eye on the slowly moving blue dot. I watched us moving too far left from the hospital. "This way," I said to Sunny, shifting to the right.

"Masha, wait."

"No, let's go," I said. I tried to move faster so I could tell exactly which way the blue dot was going.

"But, Masha!"

"Come on," I said, tripping over a low little fence. "It's this way."

QUACK . . . QUACK, QUACK, QUACK.

I fumbled my phone, and just as I got a good grip on it, the green grass beneath me disappeared and everything went black.

Six Feet Under

I stumbled about on my knees. The ground was soft under my hands. From somewhere, Sunny was calling my name, but I couldn't see anything. All around me was darkness.

QUACK . . . QUACK, QUACK, QUACK.

My phone . . . it glowed from a foot away. I reached for it, and my hand sunk into something wet. I picked up my phone. Yuck, mud. Where the heck was I?

QUACK . . . QUACK, QUACK, QUACK.

Something caught my eye. There was light over my head. I stared up at the large rectangle of sky hanging a few feet above me, confused.

QUACK . . . QUACK . . . My phone finally stopped ringing.

Then I saw Sunny staring down at me. And I understood.

"Sunny!"

"Masha!"

My heart was pounding right through my chest, but the sound of Sunny's scared voice and her giant blue eyes staring down at me kept me from screaming at the top of my lungs.

"Sunny, listen," I gulped out in a quiet, steady way . . . even though I completely wanted to jump right out of my skin. "I'm fine. I fell in a grave, that's all." The word "grave" just about stole all the air from my lungs—faster than a vampire could suck your blood.

"Really?" she sobbed.

"Totally," I said. "It's not like there is a dead body down here or something." I looked around just to be sure, and my knees actually knocked together because

I was that scared. I was stuck in a dark, muddy hole alone. But there was no dead body.

"It would be in a coffin if there were a dead body down there." Sunny sniffed. "Are you standing on a coffin?"

My heart pounded even harder in my ears just thinking about standing on a coffin. "I don't know, but I don't think so," I squeaked. "It feels soft and muddy down here."

"Probably the hole is empty and they aren't going to bury the person until another day. Otherwise," she added, "they would have pushed all the dirt back in, right?"

"Right, right, of course," I said, happy for the first time in my life to admit that Sunny knew everything.

"Anyway, it doesn't matter if there is one down there or not, Masha. It's not like dead bodies can hurt you. Zombies aren't real."

What little hair I had stood straight off my head at the thought of a zombie hand sticking out of the mud and grabbing my ankle. I stretched toward Sunny with one hand, and she reached down. Our fingers touched, and I squeezed her tiny fingertips. They felt cold. I stretched up a little farther, and we grabbed hands. "Can you pull me up?"

Sunny pulled, and I tried to stick my toes into the dirt of the side of the hole and climb out. But my cast dragged me down, and I could feel myself pulling Sunny in with me. I let go. I was stuck.

"If only we wrapped our dead and placed them up in trees like early tribes did in Australia and Siberia," she said. "Then you wouldn't be in this hole right now."

"But then we would have been walking under all the dead bodies in the trees today," I pointed out.

"Probably not," she said. "We would just have been walking on top of the bones, which would have fallen from the trees. Vultures and other scavengers would have eaten all the flesh."

"Sunny, please don't say words like 'flesh' right now." She always had to take things too far. "Listen," I said, trying to sound calm. "Go look around for a branch or something. Anything I can use to stand on or to climb out of here."

"Okay," she said.

"Wait," I told her. "Don't go more than thirty feet away from this spot."

"Why not?" she asked.

"Because I said so," I told her, sounding very much like my mother.

"Okay, Masha."

Sunny vanished from the rectangle of light above

my head, and I coughed to clear the clogged-up feeling in my throat. Pictures of forests filled with dead bodies hanging from trees floated about in my mind. I shifted to the very center of the hole to get away from the scary walls of dirt around me. Both my sneaker and my sock were each an inch deep in mud. And just because I had no better idea, I closed my eyes and clicked my muddy heels together and whispered the words, "There's no place like home. There's no place like home. There's no pla—"

I thought I heard something snap. My eyes sprang open, and my head swiveled around on my neck, taking in every nook and cranny of my hole, searching for movement. I saw none. But this didn't stop me from imagining the zombie's red fleshy arm reaching up from below my feet and pulling me deep into the mud, or picturing hundreds and thousands of beetles, with their ink-black shells and long pinching heads, crawling out from the four dirt walls surrounding me.

QUACK . . . QUACK, QUACK, QUACK.

I leaped in fear and let go of my phone. It hit the floor of the grave with a wet thud.

In Too Deep

Where are you?" shouted a voice.

"Alice?" My phone was slimy with mud. I wiped it off on my hat.

"I waited forever!" She sounded upset.

"I need help," I whispered.

"I need help," she said.

"What?"

"I said I need help," Alice repeated.

"I just said that."

"Said what?" she asked.

"Never mind," I said. "What's wrong? Where are you?"

"Why didn't you answer your phone?" she asked. "I called, and well, don't get mad," she said.

"Of course I won't. Where are you?"

"I'm in the graveyard," she answered. "And I've been out here all alone waiting on the main road for you guys for forever, and I'm freaking out. Where are you?"

"Alice," I yelped. "Alice, I'm so happy you're here. Sunny and I had an accident."

"Are you okay?"

"Hold on," I told her. "Sunny!" I shouted. "Sunny, come back."

The brim of my mother's rain hat popped over the hole.

"Stay right here," I said. "Everything's fine. Alice is here."

"In the graveyard?" she asked.

"Yes."

"In her wheelchair?"

"I guess so . . . Alice, where are you?"

"Where are you?" she asked.

"I fell in a grave."

There was silence.

"Alice?"

"You what?"

"I fell into a grave."

"How could that happen?"

"I don't know, I was watching the blue dot, and . . ."

"What blue dot?"

"On my phone. Never mind, where are you?"

"I'm on Hazel Lane," she said.

"Um," I said.

"We should have taken a map at the gate," Sunny said.

"Okay," I shouted up at her. "You're right. You are always right! I should have taken the stupid map."

"You don't have a map of the cemetery?" Alice asked.

"No, I don't," I said.

"But why not?" Alice asked. "They have millions of them at all the gates and you can't . . ."

"Alice, I do not have a map of the cemetery," I snapped. And then to Sunny I said, "Go run to the top of that hill we just came down and flap your arms around. Maybe Alice will be able to see you."

Sunny took off.

"Really, that's your plan?" Alice said.

"Listen, I'm sitting at the bottom of a grave with mud caking on my ear from my phone and maybe about to be eaten alive by big ugly beetles. Please don't yell at me."

"I'm not yelling," said Alice. "Let me see." I could hear the crinkling of paper. "If I get on Fountain Avenue, it seems to make a circle toward the inside of the cemetery. I can zip around it and look for Sunny."

"Thanks, Alice," I said.

"NP, BFF." She laughed. "This is getting kind of fun now."

"No, it's not," I said.

She giggled. I could hear the motor on her wheelchair. "I put you on speaker," she shouted.

I smiled in my hole.

"Are you flapping?" I shouted at the square of sunlight over my head.

"Yes," I heard Sunny shout, out of breath.

"Keep flapping!"

My phone clicked. Someone else was calling me. I pulled my muddy phone from my ear. My mother's picture smiled at me from the couch in our living room on Christmas morning. Oh no.

"Alice, it's my mom calling. I'll call you back."

"What are you gonna tell her?"

It clicked again.

"I don't know," I said. "But I have to answer it or she'll freak out."

I switched over to my mother.

"Hi, Mom," I said, more like I was swallowing the words than sending them into the phone.

"Hi, sweetie. How's the fair?"

"Um, it's . . ."

"I'm having a great time too!" She giggled. *Did my mother really just giggle?* "This class is so much fun, Masha. We get to sit inside the museum directly in front of an Alexandre Benois watercolor. It's so fantastic, Masha . . . and relaxing and exciting." Then she giggled again. "Anyway, how's Sunny's experiment going?"

"Um . . ." I pulled my stocking foot out of the mud and looked around my hole.

"Did they get through the first round of picks yet?"

"The first round of picks?"

"I really hope they don't just hand her the trophy after the first round like they did last year in Pennsylvania. I didn't think it was fair to the other kids."

"Yeah, me neither," I said, glad to have something to say.

"Anyway," my mom continued, "I just called Mrs. Song. She's really looking forward to having you girls for dinner. Be sure and show up hungry, you know she loves that. And don't forget to text me when you get there. I really mean it. I have my phone sitting right next to me on vibrate. Masha, you'll text me, right?"

"Yes, Mom, of course."

"What did you guys have for lunch?"

"Hamburgers," I said.

"Okay, baby. I love you. Thanks for doing this. I really appreciate it. And I know Sunny does too. She loves to be with you, Masha. She struggles so much, you know, with being different. But around you, she gets to be just, you know, Sunny. And I can't tell you what a nice day I'm having. I really needed this."

"NP, Mom," I said, mimicking Alice.

"What, sweetie?"

"No problem, Mom, no problem," I choked.

I so wanted to scream, "HELP, I'M STUCK AT THE BOTTOM OF A GRAVE!" But I didn't. I couldn't . . . not after hearing about my mom having a great time and her giggling about it and all. I reached out and touched the dirt on the side of the grave. I could handle this.

"Okay, see you soon. Eat lots of dumplings tonight."

She smacked me a kiss and hung up.

I looked up at the large rectangle of light over my head and tears popped from my eyes and rolled into the mud on my cheeks. I was never getting us home.

And then I heard the whirring of a wheelchair motor.

Being the Load

Alice!" I cried.

"Masha!" came her reply from just outside that rectangle of light above my head.

"How deep is it?" she asked. I knew her wheelchair couldn't get too close to the hole because of the tiny black fence that surrounded it.

"Really deep," I called out.

Sunny's head popped back into view at the top of the hole. "I'd estimate it at six feet, four inches; possibly six feet, five inches."

We both ignored Sunny.

"Alice, get me out of here!"

Silence came from the top of the hole.

"Ohhhh," I wailed.

"Don't worry, Masha, I'll get you out," Alice said. "Let me think for a minute."

"Did you see anyone else in the graveyard?" I asked.

"No," she said.

"We didn't either." I groaned. "It's such a beautiful Saturday. You'd think more people would be visiting their dead grandparents!" It's funny how just a half hour ago I was so happy that there was no one in the cemetery to see Sunny's experiment—*me*—and now I was wondering where the heck everyone was.

"Maybe I can go up to the front of the graveyard. Maybe there is a guard or a policeman there," Alice suggested.

"We came in that way, and we didn't see a guard," I said. "Plus that will take so long, and I want to get out of this hole right now."

"It won't take that long. I'll only be gone for twenty minutes, tops."

"No," I shouted. "Don't leave me."

"Okay, okay, Masha. I'm right here. I won't leave you."

"We might be able to get her out using a simple machine," said Sunny.

"Like my wheelchair?" Alice asked.

"That's not a simple machine," Sunny said. "That's a complex machine."

"What other machine do we have?" I asked.

"We can make one."

"How can we make a machine in the middle of a graveyard?" Alice asked.

"A simple machine is just a device that changes the direction or magnitude of a force," Sunny said.

"Get to the point," Alice said.

I smiled in my hole. I loved Alice.

"We need a mechanical advantage to pull Masha out of there. You know, leverage. You're kind of skinny, Masha," Sunny said. "But you're still too heavy for us to just pull you out using our arms. We need a fulcrum and force, and then we can pull you out of the hole. We need to create a lever."

"Okay, let's do it," Alice said.

"I don't even get what she's talking about!" I shouted.

"Give her a chance, Masha. I'm sure we'll understand it better when she sets up what she needs."

I wasn't smiling right now, and I wasn't loving Alice so much either.

I heard mumbling going on outside my hole, and I hugged my cast to the *P* on my chest. If only I really were a superhero—a real Paintgirl could get herself out of a hole in the ground.

"What are you guys doing?" I asked. But no one answered. I checked the mud around my feet for beetles again. I swear I thought I saw something move near my sneakerless foot.

"Guys!"

"We're right here," Alice called.

"Masha," Sunny breathed down into the dark. "We found a lever." A long object poked into the hole and knocked me in the head.

"Watch out! Why are you hitting me with a stick?"

"It's a plank of wood," Sunny said. "We found it behind one of the little grave houses. You're going to hang on to the one end, and Alice and I are going to lift you out of the hole."

"How are you going to do that?" I whined.

"We're going to create a lever," Sunny said. "Alice and I will be the force. The iron fence around the grave that you tripped over will be the fulcrum. And you will be the load, Masha. If the force applied is twice the distance from the fulcrum than the load, Alice and I will only need half the effort to pull you out than if we just used our own strength!" She was looking a little too excited about this. Whenever Sunny got excited, bad things usually happened to me. I looked down at my muddy, red-splattered, broken-armed self, and I knew that nothing good was going to come from this lever thing.

"'Lever' is just another name for a seesaw, Masha," Alice called from over the top of my muddy prison. "Only the board of the seesaw is placed unevenly, with lots more seesaw board on our side. Sunny says it makes it easier to pull you out."

"Okay," I said. "Although I don't know why I have to be called a load," I grumbled.

"You have to be the load," Sunny insisted. "You're the one that needs to be moved out of the hole."

"Whatever," I said.

"Hold on to the wooden plank and get ready to be lifted," she said, her eyes glowing. And then she disappeared. My hands tried to grip the wood, but it was too wide to really hang on to. Instead, I threw my cast and my good arm over it so I was holding on with both my elbows. I cringed, ready for something to happen but not wanting it to. I was just about to call out to Alice and Sunny to ask what was supposed to be happening when the wood jerked in my arms.

I held on, which wasn't so easy with my cast.

My arms, wrapped around the plank, shot up over my head. My good arm shot higher than the arm with the cast on it, jerking me into a weird position.

And then both my arms felt like they were being pulled from their sockets. Before I could think, my feet lifted out of the mud and dangled below me.

I held on.

Within seconds my head was even with the hole. I blinked in the sunlight. Alice was leaning out of her wheelchair and Sunny was standing next to her, and both of them were pushing down on the

other side of the long piece of wood, huge smiles on their faces. I couldn't believe it—it was working!

"Now what?" I cried, huffing and puffing and trying to cling to the plank.

"What are you kids doing?" someone growled.

And . . . *plop!* I was on my butt in the mud again.

Three of a Kind

I really did fall in by accident. We weren't playing around," I said for the sixty-millionth time in three minutes.

"Listen," said the gardener. "I don't know what you girls are doing running around in here without your parents. This isn't a playground. You're lucky I had my pruning ladder with me today."

I looked down at the muddy mess that was me. "I would have been luckier if you'd come along before the whole lever thing," I said.

"I'm going to call security," he said, pulling a radio out of his tool belt.

"No need for that. My mom's waiting for us by the back gate to the hospital," Alice said, covering for me. "Thanks so much for your help." She motioned for Sunny and me to follow her.

He nodded in her direction but didn't look directly at her, and he didn't say anything at first. And then he said, "Well, okay, get along." It seems that he didn't have a problem treating me badly, but he couldn't treat Alice that way.

"My brother and I call it 'blinky-eye,'" explained Alice, when he was gone and we were back on Fountain Avenue trudging toward the back gate that stood across the street from the hospital. "Because of the spina bifida, I don't look like a regular person." She snorted. "So people do a lot of blinking so they don't have to actually see me. And then they give me anything I want and hurry away."

"You do too look like a regular person," I said.

"And the people that don't get all blinky with me pat me on the head and speak really loudly and slowly to me," she continued, "like I'm some old dog that doesn't hear very well!"

"People may behave that way because your outward appearance is different, and that leads to them to believe that your inward appearance is also different," Sunny stated in her annoying scientific tone while she swung her bucket of fly eggs at her side. "You know, like your mind may not be . . . regular."

"Sunny!" I said.

"No, Masha. Let her talk. I want to hear more." Alice spun her wheelchair around to a stop in front of Sunny. Her dark eyes that always seemed so ready to laugh at everything stared hard, like they were not so ready to hear what Sunny had to say. The late-afternoon sun created a red halo glow over the top of her black hair.

"Look at Masha," Sunny said. "I made Masha look different with red dye. You were born looking different. Either way, neither of you looks like everyone else, even if you don't mean to. Didn't you notice, Masha," Sunny continued, looking over at me, "how Jeremy's mom didn't really want to answer your question about which bus we were on? It's the same thing as the gardener not wanting to look at Alice. You and Alice look different. And looking different makes people think you *are* different."

"Like the janitor at the science fair," I said. "He told me I didn't belong, and he was right."

Alice hiccupped and stared down into her lap. Then tears began to drop from under her dark eyelashes.

I ran to her.

"I don't want to be different," Alice cried.

"You're not, Alice," I said. "Sunny doesn't know what she's talking about."

"Of course I know what I'm talking a—" Sunny started.

"Sunny!" I hissed. "Enough."

"I dream of having a beautiful, strong spine," Alice spit through the waterfall rolling over her cheeks and into her mouth. "I picture all the bony vertebrae lining up neatly in a long, straight row. I picture them moving together as I walk down the street." She looked out over the tops of the trees as she spoke. "Sometimes," she said, looking back at Sunny and

me, "I think about it so hard that I almost feel like I can make it happen just because I want it that badly. But it doesn't ever happen." Then Alice looked right at me. "I want to be regular, Masha," she said. And then she hung her head. "I don't want to be . . . different!"

"You're not different," I said, hugging her pony-tailed head to my chest. The three of us formed a little circle in the center of a tiny cemetery road wrongly named Joy Path.

I saw Sunny take a breath to say something, and I shot her a "you better not open your mouth" look.

"I am too," sniffed Alice into my shirt. "It's just like Sunny said."

"Sunny doesn't know everything," I told her while I stared Sunny down.

"Well, 'everything' is not really a true measurement," Sunny mumbled, hugging the paint can to her chest.

I made a growling face at her.

"Anyway, Alice," I said, unhugging her head and looking her right in the eyes, "people should look at you. And I mean *really* look at you. Because the you that I see is totally beautiful."

Alice turned a little away from me, wiping her face with the palms of her hands. "Would you be mad if I told you that I want to be beautiful to everyone and not just to you, Masha?" she said.

I shook my head no. "Of course I wouldn't," I whispered. My lungs felt like two tubes of toothpaste being squeezed tight, and my eyes let go of a bunch of tears. "I know that teachers and moms say that it's the inside that counts and all, but I want to be beautiful on the outside too. Everybody does."

"I don't," Sunny said.

Alice and I looked up at Sunny. She looked back at us. "What?" she said. "I don't."

We turned back to each other and started to laugh.

"What is so funny?" she asked. My little sister didn't really get why Alice had cried, and now she didn't understand why we were laughing. As always, the word "weird" popped into my head to sum up Sunny. But this time the word didn't exactly sum her up. When I realized what did, it made my heart burn in my chest.

Different.

All three of us . . . We were all different.

A Wet Wedding, a Real Wedding, and No Bus

The lever would have worked," Sunny mumbled, scraping and clomping along in her boot and my sneaker.

"I'm sure it would have," I said, glancing at Alice. Our eyes met. We could tell that Sunny was still feeling hurt over us laughing.

"Want to ride in my lap?" Alice asked her as a way of apologizing.

"Yeah," cried Sunny, jumping up and down like the little six-year-old that she was. She scrambled into Alice's wheelchair with her paint can. We rolled along the little cemetery roads. Sunny read Alice's map, and we made the rights and lefts that she told us to. The sun shone from a little bit of a distance but still felt warm on my shoulders. The trees were as green as shamrocks, and everywhere I looked were these bushes covered in tiny yellow flowers that reminded me of a firework explosion frozen in place. I took in a big breath of graveyard air. It felt great to be out of that hole. I swung my arms just because I could and glanced at the tops of the trees where they met the blue sky. All of a sudden I remembered the dead bodies hanging in the tree branches that Sunny told me about. I kind of hoped that she made that up, but Sunny never made anything up. And then I remembered where we were supposed to be today.

"Hey Sunny, are you upset about missing the science fair?" I asked.

Sunny pulled out her phone and checked the time.

"Why do you keep caring about the time?" I asked.

Sunny just shrugged.

That was weird. Not having an answer is not like my little sister.

"Is there something in that paint can, Sunny? It kind of smells. And why don't you take off the rain hat?" Alice asked. "Aren't you hot?"

"I'm fine," Sunny said, pulling the hat down tighter onto her head and the paint can closer to her chest.

Now I was getting suspicious. "What's up with that hat?" I asked. "You are way too attached to it today." I swiped at it and Sunny dodged me, almost cracking her head into Alice's head.

"Stop, Masha," Sunny cried.

"Just take it off," I said.

"No," she answered.

"Come on. Do it."

"No. It's my hat."

"It's Mom's hat."

"Guys," Alice said, stopping her wheelchair. "What does it matter that Sunny won't take off the hat, Masha? You've got a hat on too. And is that a *P* on your T-shirt?" she asked.

I quickly pulled my cast to my chest to cover the "P." I was a little hurt that Alice took Sunny's side. "The difference between my hat and hers," I said,

ignoring the "P" comment, "is that she's up to something with hers. I know my little sister. And whatever
it is that Sunny is up to, it isn't good for me."

"Are you up to something with your hat, Sunny?"
Alice asked her.

"I don't understand the question," Sunny said, avoiding Alice's eyes.

"You've never *not* understood anything in your life," I shouted. "You are totally up to something."

"What could she possibly be doing with a hat?" Alice asked.

I stared down at Sunny sitting on Alice's lap. Sunny stared up at me.

And then she smiled.

I leaped at her throat.

"Masha!" cried Alice, muffled by my body. "Get off. You're getting mud all over us."

I got off, still breathing heavily from my attempt to strangle my little sister.

"Okay," Alice said. "Let's talk about some other piece of clothing. Why are you wearing Masha's sneaker? Where's your boot?"

"Masha threw it up onto the roof," Sunny said, trying not to smile again.

"After she did this!" I yelled, gesturing at the red dye. "And if you're going to get a ride the whole way to the hospital, give me back my sneaker."

Sunny plucked off my sneaker and threw it to the side of the road using one hand while holding onto her stupid rain hat with the other hand.

"I'm not going to touch your stupid hat," I snapped, going for my sneaker. "In fact, you can wear that hat to your stinkin' wedding! I couldn't care less."

Sunny and Alice giggled.

"She'd have to wear high-heeled rain boots," Alice said.

"And I could carry an umbrella instead of a bunch of flowers," laughed Sunny.

"We'd all throw buckets of water at her instead of rice," I grumbled.

"You could release ducks into the air instead of doves," giggled Alice.

"And my honeymoon would be to the rainforest," Sunny added.

We were all laughing when we came around a corner and saw a group of people huddled together under two trees by a large flowered area—a real wedding! All fifty or so pairs of eyes were staring over at us. And all fifty or so mouths were twisted down into a frown. We made our way past them as fast as we could without breaking down in laughter. Once we got over a small hill, Alice burst out, "Who would get married in a graveyard?"

We couldn't hold it in any longer. We exploded into giggles . . . forgetting all about Sunny Sweet's rain hat as we headed out of the cemetery through another set of giant, black iron gates.

"I don't want to go back to the hospital," Alice said. The hospital was across the street, with the front entrance just down a half a block. "This was so much fun!"

"Really?" I said, motioning at my red-speckled, muddy self. "This isn't much fun."

"Well, for me it was fun." She laughed. "Except maybe for the part where I was alone in the grave-yard. That part wasn't fun."

"When the gardener ruined my lever experiment," Sunny said, "that wasn't any fun for me."

"Yeah, for me either," I said. And we all laughed.

"I love hanging out with you two." Alice sighed.

"I'm going to pin up the cemetery map right next to my bed," she said, smoothing out its wrinkles.

Sunny looked over at me and smiled. I smiled back.

We walked Alice to the front door of the hospital. "Where will you tell them that you've been?" I asked.

"I told the nurse that I was going to read to the patients in geriatrics, so nobody is even looking for me. If they were, the nurse would have texted me."

"What's geriatrics?" I asked.

"Old people," said Sunny.

"Why would you read to old people? Why don't they just read to themselves?"

"Lots of times they can't read anymore because their eyes are bad. Or they're too sick. I like to go read to them anyway. It's fun."

"So you really do read to them? It wasn't just an excuse to get out today?"

"No, I really do it. Not today . . . Today I had to go dig my friend out of an early grave," she laughed. "But other days I do. This week I am reading them *Harry Potter and the Goblet of Fire*."

"That's cool," I said. "Maybe I can come listen one day." We were in front of the doors to the hospital. I gave her a hug. After I stood back up, I saw the old Alice looking at me, the Alice who could handle anything. Maybe being near the hospital made her strong. "I wish you could come home with us, Alice," I said.

"And eat some of Mrs. Song's dumplings," Sunny added.

"Me too," she sighed.

"Sunny and I will visit you one day this week. That is, if I can get us home without my mom finding out about any of this. Otherwise, she'll never let me out alone again for the rest of my life!"

"Okay," Alice said. "Then get home."

Home. It was like it had become some mystical place that didn't really exist anymore. "I've been trying all day." I sighed. "Anyway . . ." I gave her wheelchair wheel a little kick. "Thanks for saving me, best friend."

Alice winked. I loved when she did that. She's the only kid I knew who did that.

Sunny squeezed Alice around the arms and then crawled off her. "Yeah, Alice, thanks for helping us."

"Hey," she smiled before she turned and rolled in through the automatic doors, "we're like Harry, Ron, and Hermione. Although instead of being wizards, we're just weird."

"You can be Ron," I shouted after her. I heard her laugh before the doors shut.

Sunny and I turned and headed back for the bus stop and the number 68.

"What did she mean by weird?" Sunny asked.

"You know, that the three of us are all different, just like you said."

"I'm not different," Sunny said.

I looked over at Sunny, making a point to look at her big rain hat and her feet, with one socked foot and one foot in a rain boot, and the paint can in her hand filled with a half-eaten hamburger loaded down with fly eggs. And then there was the whole being-a-genius thing, which definitely made Sunny different. "And I thought you were the smart one," I told her.

She was quiet.

"I'm just teasing, Sunny."

We walked to the bench at the bus stop and sat down. We sat for a while staring off down the street. A bus came. It was the 66. Two more 66 buses came, but there was no sign of the 68.

"So are you really sad about the science fair?" I asked. "You never answered me. This will be the very first contest I ever saw you enter that you won't win."

She shrugged.

Again I did not like the shrug. It made me nervous.

"This will be your first time as a loser," I told her, trying to get her mad.

Again she shrugged.

"Stop doing that," I snapped. "And take off that stupid rain hat!"

She leaped off the bench, and I jumped off after her. I chased her around the bench. Just as I had her bucket of fly eggs within reach, I heard the engine of a bus roaring up the street. I stopped chasing Sunny and scooted over to the curb, straining to get a look at which bus it was. Another 66!

I stomped over to the bus stop sign and squinted at the schedule. Maybe the 68 only came once every half hour or something. Sunny came up and stood next to me.

"It says that it should come every ten minutes," I said.

"Except on weekends," noted Sunny, pointing to a horrible red line that ran down the length of the schedule under the words "Saturday and Sundays."

I let out a very heavy sigh. "Figures."

It Ain't Over Until . . .
Never, Because the Universe
Is Always Expanding

Sunny checked the time on her phone.

"What time is it?" I asked her.

"It's three p.m.," she said.

"I'd better text Mom."

"What are you gonna tell her?" Sunny asked. Her eyes were staring out into the world, but I could tell they were really staring back into that giant brain of hers and doing calculations of some sort.

"That the fair is almost over and we'll be getting on the bus soon."

"You're gonna lie?"

I sat down on the bench and put my head in my hands.

"I'm sorry, Masha," Sunny said, sitting down next to me. "Why don't you text her that everything is good. That's not a lie."

"That's not a lie?" I asked. "Look at us, Sunny. We're stuck at the hospital. I'm covered with red junk and mud, and you're wearing one boot and carrying a can of old meat. Are things really good?" I looked over at her. Her mouth was turned down in a tiny frown.

I looked around me at the big pots of flowers and the bench I sat on. This bus stop was the place where I'd first seen Sunny bald after she'd glued those flowers to my head and we both had our heads shaved. This hospital was the very place where she had said that she was sorry to me for the first time ever in our lives. And believe me, there had been ten million other times that Sunny Sweet should have said those words to me.

Sunny's phone buzzed. "It's Mom," she said. "She sent a picture." Sunny turned the phone so I could see. It was a picture of my mother's watercolor in progress. I looked up at Sunny, and we smiled.

"It's pretty," I said.

Pretty, Sunny texted.

"Hey," I said. "Let's take a selfie and send it to her."

"What about the red dye all over your face?"

"She'll be seeing it soon enough," I said.

We stuck our heads together, hat to hat, and smiled for the camera. I held Sunny's phone away from us to snap it. Then I checked to be sure that our heads completely filled the screen so you couldn't tell where we were. Sunny and I grinned out at me from her phone. I was indeed a picture of red splotchiness, but we looked happy—like we weren't stuck on a bench.

I texted, The red paint is part of Sunny's experiment, and then clicked Send.

Pretty? my mom texted back, followed by like a thousand smileys. She loves those silly yellow faces.

I handed Sunny's phone back to her and gave her hand a little squeeze.

She clicked on the picture of the two of us and stared at it. "Am I really different too?" she asked.

It wasn't so often that Sunny asked me a question she didn't already know the answer to.

"Yes," I told her.

She nodded.

We sat on the bench together in silence except for when someone walked by. And then I'd put my cell phone to my ear and say loudly, "Yes, Mom, we're sitting right here on the bench in the front and we won't move an inch." I didn't want anyone asking us where our parents were.

Each person that passed noticed us. They all tried to hide it, but there is something about eyes that make them really hard to miss. They glow. The first look always came with that eye-opening surprise. And then they'd swerve their eyes away for a moment, maybe to figure out what they just saw. Then their eyes would come back, like they couldn't stop from taking another look. I guess they did it in a hidden way because it's rude to stare at people. But I could tell that they also hid it because they didn't want me or Sunny saying something to them. Anyway, they didn't have to worry. You couldn't catch spina bifida—or what Sunny and I had, which was a very bad case of a way-too-stinkin'-smart-little-sister—like you caught a cold.

A lady wearing a black-and-white-checked jacket walked by with a small, fluffy dog in a black-and-white-checked sweater. I'd never seen anyone match her dog before. When they got about two feet away, I did my fake-conversation thing with my mom and Sunny reached down to pet her dog. The lady caught sight of me and yanked the dog away before Sunny's hand could touch it. Then she hurried down the street, dragging the little dog with her. Sunny and I scooted closer to one another on the bench.

"Dumb lady," I said.

"She just doesn't understand us," Sunny said.

"So does that give her the right to treat us badly?" I said.

"People are afraid of differences," Sunny explained.

"Well, then, they're dumb," I said.

"Not necessarily. Sometimes it's important to be aware of stuff that is different. It can keep you safe."

"We're not going to hurt anybody," I snapped. "And what about Alice? She isn't going to hurt anybody either."

"That's true," Sunny said. "But people don't understand spina bifida. They don't understand that Alice's backbone and spinal canal did not close before birth. And they don't understand that because of this, Alice can't move her muscles the way other people can. And because they don't understand, they're afraid of her."

"So," I said, because truthfully, I hadn't understood any of that stuff either, "if people understood why Alice looked different, they wouldn't be afraid."

"That's right," Sunny said. "They wouldn't be afraid."

"And this is what your experiment for the fair is all about?" I asked. "If we knew why people looked and acted differently, we wouldn't be afraid of them?"

"Pretty much, yes," she said, reaching up and adjusting the rain hat solidly onto her head. "My hypothesis is that the more we understand what makes others different from ourselves, the less those differences will matter."

I thought about Batman and Robin back at the school, and how no one even looked at them funny. Everybody at that school understood that the boys wanted to be superheroes. In fact, maybe everyone in the world understood Batman and Robin. But a red-speckled girl like me, or a kid with spina bifida, they just needed more explanation.

I leaped off the bench and pulled out my cell phone and dialed.

"Who are you calling?"

"I'm calling Junchao at the science fair." The phone kept ringing.

"Why?" Sunny asked.

"To see if we can still make it," I told her.

Sunny jumped off the bench, pulling out her own phone. She took a look at the screen and then looked up at me, her eyes shining. "We can make it!"

I had no idea how she knew, but I never knew how she knew anything. I clicked off my phone, grabbed Sunny's hand, and started to run.

"Back through the graveyard?" Sunny asked, already out of breath.

"Yup," I said, laughing. "And this time, we take a map!"

Graveyards Are Scary

Do you see him?" Sunny asked.

I peeked through the gate of the cemetery but didn't see the gardener or anyone. "No, come on."

We scurried through the gate and over to the little shed that held the maps. Sunny grabbed a map, and I pulled her around the back of the tiny building while we read it.

"It looks like we need to take Poplar Avenue to Walnut Avenue to Spruce Street. This will take us back to the gate by The Mug."

"Let's go," I said.

Sunny folded up the map and stuck it in her jeans pocket.

"Good job." I smiled.

I stuck my head out from behind the shed and looked around. I saw no one. It was getting pretty late in the afternoon, and the trees were making shadows across the darkening grass. They didn't look like broccoli anymore, but like dark figures waiting to grab us as we ran by. The headstones, which just an hour ago had looked like friendly rocks sunning themselves on a spring afternoon, now looked cold and hard. All of a sudden the cemetery seemed a little spooky to me.

"What's the matter?" asked Sunny.

"Uh . . . uh," I stammered. "Nothing."

"Did you see something?"

My heart jumped at her words. "No," I said, staring down at her. "Did you?"

Her eyes grew big.

"Never mind," I told her. "Let's just run."

We took off down Poplar Avenue. I could see the road twisting ahead of me and knew that if we cut across the graves we'd get there faster, but I wasn't about to do that now. The idea of running over graves completely freaked me out. Sunny was running next to me. I could hear her breathing heavily so I slowed down a little. Then something caught my eye.

I leaped to the opposite side of Poplar Avenue, pulling Sunny with me. We ducked behind a gravestone.

"What?" she asked.

I looked all around us. "It wasn't anything, I guess."

Somewhere behind us a leaf blower started and we grabbed each other in a hug.

"How far is Walnut Avenue from here?" I whispered.

Sunny pulled out the map. "I'm not sure," she said.

"Why are you sure about everything always until we get stuck in the middle of a graveyard?" I asked. "Never mind." I took her hand and we got back on the path and started running again. We passed Laurel Mountain Road and then Fern Place. I was completely out of breath by the time we got to Walnut Avenue.

"I'm tired," Sunny said, stopping in the middle of the little intersection of Poplar and Walnut.

"We have to keep going."

"I don't want to run anymore. My legs hurt. And it's hard to run with just one boot."

"Well, maybe if you put down that stupid bucket it might be easier."

She hugged the can of fly eggs to her chest protectively.

I rolled my eyes. "Sunny Sweet, we can get you more fly eggs another day."

"But I've been carrying them all day. They're like my babies."

"Hey!" cried a voice. It was the gardener.

Sunny tossed her fly babies onto the grass, kicked off her rain boot, and we took off.

We didn't hesitate when we saw Spruce Avenue. We turned down the path, running at full speed for the tall, dark gate at the end of it. I ached to look back, but I was running too fast. We ran straight out the gate, across The Mug's parking lot, and into the door of the coffee shop without stopping.

We stood right inside the doors, breathing. No one even looked up from their laptops. I glanced over at

the baristas. They were busy fiddling with machines and wiping counters. Sunny and I stuck our noses to the glass doors and peered out at the cemetery gate. It stood black and heavy over the entrance to the graveyard. We kept staring. No one came out of the gate. We looked at one another and then back at the gate. Still no one.

"Excuse me," someone asked from behind us.

Sunny and I jumped, smashing into the glass doors.

A girl a little older than babysitting age was standing behind us. "Excuse me," she said.

"Yeah, no one's chasing us," I stammered. I think I smiled at her, but I was shaking so hard that I'm not sure that I did.

"But I had to throw away my fly eggs," Sunny told her.

She gave us Alice's "blinky-eye," where she just blinked a lot and didn't really look at us, and then she hurried past us and out the door. We watched her go. And then I saw it—the bus. Sunny saw it too. We took off out the door and down the sidewalk of the coffee shop, screeching to a halt under the bus sign.

"What's the name of the high school where the fair is, Sunny?"

"Highland Latin," she said.

The bus came to a stop in front of us. The doors opened. I was scared it was going to be the same driver, but it wasn't. "Do you stop at Highland Latin School?" I asked him.

"I stop three blocks away, on Marlboro and West Sudbury," he said.

"That's the hamburger stop," Sunny said excitedly.

"Don't get any ideas," I told her as we climbed on. But I knew she was getting ideas. She always got ideas.

Masha Sweet Is
a Winner

I texted my mom that the fair was almost over and that I hoped she was having a good day. Then I stared out the window as we drove along the street with the bus's motor roaring underneath us. I didn't stare outside the bus because I didn't want to notice how everyone on the bus had just moved away from Sunny and me when we sat down; I stared outside the bus because I wasn't going to miss the Marlboro and West Sudbury stop.

Sunny swung her feet under her seat. Her socks were black with dirt.

"Do you want my sneakers?" I asked, looking back out the bus window.

"No," she said. And then she changed her mind. "I mean, yes."

I took off my sneakers and handed them to her.

My feet were still damp and cold from the muddy grave. I pulled my socks up as best I could and settled back to watch for our stop.

Out of the corner of my eye I watched Sunny put one of my sneakers on very slowly and then she very quietly placed the other one on her lap. It took me a second to understand why . . . but then I got it. I took both eyes from the window and glared down at her. "Why are you not putting that shoe on? And don't think that I don't know the answer to my own question, because I do," I shouted.

The people who were sneakily staring at us quickly turned away.

"I don't know what you're . . . ," Sunny started.

I grabbed at my sneaker but she was faster, and she whisked it off her lap and held it out in the aisle of the bus.

"Give it to me."

"No."

"Why not? Why won't you give it to me?" I asked reaching across her while she dangled the sneaker farther away.

"I need it."

"For what? And I know for what—for more fly eggs!"

"I need them, Masha. I'm going to do an experiment."

"You are right in the middle of an experiment," I yelled at her. "Why don't you just worry about this one?" I yelled, pointing at myself.

"I'm just gonna—"

"SUNNY SWEET, YOU ARE SO NOT PUTTING DOG POOP IN MY SHOE!"

"Okay," said the bus driver. "Calm down back there."

I threw myself back into my seat and stared out the window. Otherwise, I might pick Sunny up and toss her down the aisle of the bus. And that's when I saw it . . . our stop.

My first reaction was to jump at the yellow strip and press. But then I had an idea—no stop, no dog poop. I slid a little deeper into my seat and glanced over at Sunny. She still had my sneaker over on her right side, where I couldn't get it. I smiled.

Then I heard the ding of the stop signal.

Someone else had pushed it.

Just stay still and quiet, I told myself. *Don't move, don't breathe, and we'll slide on by that horrible stop and I'll win!*

I held my breath and stared straight ahead as the bus came to a stop and the doors flew open.

Sunny glanced over at me. Then she looked right at me. And then she leaped up and sprang for the doors. Fried fiddlesticks!

I leaped up and hopped off the bus after her, jumping in between her and the fly eggs. The bus driver closed the doors with a thump and then gunned the bus engine, leaving Sunny and me coughing in the exhaust.

"If you take one step toward that, the . . . eggs," I warned, "you will be dead meat!"

"Masha . . . ," she started.

"Dead meat," I repeated.

"M—"

"Dead meat," I interrupted.

Sunny's cell phone blinged with a text. She checked

it. "Okay," she said. "We have to get to the school now."

"Toss me my shoes," I said.

She thought for a second and then tossed me the sneaker in her hand.

"Both of them," I said, standing taller and placing my hands on my hips.

It just goes to show you how smart my little sister is, because she tossed me my other sneaker. Sunny Sweet was so *not* winning this battle, and she knew it.

I missed both of her tosses but quickly picked up my sneakers and stuck them back on my damp feet.

Sunny looked at her cell phone. "We have to run," she said.

Sunny and I started running for the school. Sunny was running so fast that she had to hold onto her hat so it wouldn't fly off her head. But I didn't care about the stupid hat anymore. I had just won a fight with Sunny Sweet! I won. *Masha Sweet is a winner.* I bounced along in my dusty, muddy, ketchupy clothes, my orange cast at my side and the little growing hairs under my slouchy knit hat. I would get Sunny Sweet to the fair in time for her to win, and then I'd get us both home safely afterward to eat dumplings with Mrs. Song, and in the end, I'd make my mother proud. I felt strong and in control. It was like I could feel the *P* on my chest light up. I was Paintgirl, and everything was going my way.

Being the Experiment, Really Being It

We ran back across the parking lot where the ketchup bottle had exploded. And then we ran under Sunny's tree to the front doors of the school.

Once inside, I caught my breath while Sunny asked the first official-looking adult who we saw if they had given out the awards. She was cleaning up a bake sale table.

"The judges are just getting on the stage now," she said, as she dropped a bunch of paper plates into the garbage.

We started past her.

"Wait," she said, straightening up and looking at us. "You're the little girl with the camera. Wonderful." She nodded and smiled. "You need to get around the back and head up the stage steps."

"Which way?" Sunny asked. And the lady pointed to her left and down a hall.

We followed her pointed finger and took off.

"What did she mean," I huffed, "by the camera?" All this running was starting to catch up with me, but Sunny seemed like she'd caught a second wind. She was ten steps ahead of me and moving fast.

We came to the auditorium door first. Sunny opened it, peeked inside, and then shut it. I caught up to her. "What?"

"This way," she said, heading to the next door. It read STAGE DOOR.

I pulled it open for her, and she danced through it.

It was dark. We could see the stage lights up a small staircase, and we followed the steps up toward the light. There were a few dim figures moving about on the side of the stage. They all seemed to be watching us as we came up the stairs. It was as if they had been waiting for us. But all day long people had been looking at me. I was so over it that I didn't bother to look back. They parted for us as we got closer, and the bright lights of the stage blinded me.

After a second my eyes adjusted and out on the stage under the lights I could see the judges speaking to the crowd. I could hear their voices too, but I couldn't hear what they were saying. Sunny walked right up to the side of the curtain and peered out at them. I followed her.

"And here they are now," said the one judge, looking right at Sunny and me and smiling.

I looked behind me. Who was he talking about?

One of the dim figures from backstage put his arms around Sunny and me, and before I knew it, I was being walked out onto the stage with my little sister.

Sunny stood next to the judges in her stocking feet, smiling. They handed her a giant trophy. She looked so natural, standing on the stage accepting a trophy, like she did it every day, which I guess wasn't that far from the truth. But how was she winning this one?

We'd been in the building for only four minutes. I stood next to her trying to get my mouth to close while an entire crowd of people stared up at me. But then I noticed that they weren't quite staring at me. They were staring behind me.

I followed their eyes to a huge screen on the stage behind me.

At first I didn't recognize myself all clean, without the mud and dust and red splotches. I might have been able to deny it was me except there on my arm was the orange cast and on my head was my red knit hat! And what was I doing? I was marching across the parking lot carrying Sunny Sweet's box with her science experiment. What? My life was a movie? But how?

I looked over at Sunny. She took off her rain hat and bowed to the crowd and I understood. The hat . . . There was a camera in her hat. She had filmed the entire day!

Sunny Sweet's face was lit up like a gas station at night as the crowd applauded her. My brain whirred in my head, trying to catch me up to what was happening. My poor brain was taking up so much energy trying to understand my situation that my legs wobbled and almost dropped me onto the stage floor.

She filmed me getting on the wrong bus . . . and me not taking a map . . . and me falling into a grave. I looked behind me at the giant screen, playing my day.

There I was, opening the ketchup bottle. *Pop!* And there I was covered in red splotches. The crowd burst out laughing.

The judges on the stage surrounded Sunny and me, pulling us into a line with their arms around our shoulders. "Here are the little girls we've been watching all day long," said one of the judges who held a microphone. "Today we've seen some of Sonya Sweet's groundbreaking work in social behavior, and I have no doubt that the future of science is bright."

The crowd applauded.

"Just a couple of pictures, girls," said someone offstage.

I looked out into the crowd. A camera flash lit up in my eyes. When I refocused, I was staring down at Michael Capezzi. He gave a little wave, and I felt like I had swallowed Sunny's half-eaten hamburger and the fly eggs were hatching in my stomach. I glanced over at my smiling little sister. I decided right then and there that Sunny Sweet was most definitely dead meat!

One of the judges walked Sunny and her trophy

up to the center of the stage in front of the microphone. "We are happy to award the first place science trophy to Sonya Sweet for her work on social behavior in action."

Everyone clapped. I rolled my eyes.

Sunny stood on her tippy toes to reach the microphone. "Thank you for this award," she said.

Again the crowd clapped.

"A lot of work and planning went into my experiment today," she continued, and then she looked back at me. "But I couldn't have done any of it without my sister, Masha. You have to be brave to be different. And my big sister is very brave."

The crowd clapped and clapped and clapped. I gave a quick bow, and they clapped even harder.

Okay, maybe dead meat was going too far. Maybe I'd just kick Sunny Sweet really hard in the shin.

With that settled . . . I took another bow.

Being a Superhero

I had to endure a longer photo session offstage once the award ceremony was over. And when that finished, there were the endless congratulations from the judges. I'd seen this part of a science fair way too many times and whispered to Sunny that I was going to the bathroom.

"Number one or number two?" She giggled.

I glared at her and walked away.

Everybody was packing up and leaving. Kids were putting metal and wires and cardboard junk into boxes, and adults were standing around talking to one another.

No one even gave me a second look as I passed. It was just as Sunny said it would be. As soon as everyone understood why I looked like I did—all full of ketchup and mud and dust and stuff—they were no longer afraid of me . . . or even that interested. I was just a kid whose little sister abused her in the name of science.

I saw the sign for the bathroom and followed it around the corner, where I bumped right into the janitor. I spun around and started to walk away, but he called out to me.

"Hey, kid, wait."

I kept going.

"Wait!" he shouted.

I stopped and turned around. "I was just going to go to the bathroom," I explained. "And then I swear I'm leaving, and I promise never to come back."

"No, I mean, sure, but wait. I wanted to, er, ask about that girl in the wheelchair," he said. "She has spina bifida, right?"

"You mean my friend Alice?" I asked. "Yes, she does."

He looked down at the shine on the hallway floor

and nodded his head, thinking about something, I guess. And then he said, "My little girl has spina bifida too."

"Wow, that is so cool!" I said.

He grinned. "You know, no one has ever said that before."

"Does she go to school here?" I asked.

"No, no. But she did. She graduated quite a few years ago. She's a librarian, at the Parker Hill branch of the public library."

"Really?" I said. "Maybe Alice and I can visit her one day."

"I think she'd like that," he said, his eyes twinkling. And then his eyes stopped their twinkling and narrowed on me. "I'm sorry I was a bit grumpy earlier today. These science fairs turn me into a wreck."

"Yeah, they do the same thing to me," I said, looking down at myself.

We laughed.

"And hey, kid," he said, getting serious again, "you did belong here. I guess we all do." He shrugged. He gave me a little nod and then turned and walked away.

I stood where I was for a second and watched his keys jingle at his side as he walked off down the hall. He was right. We all did belong. Finding out how, now that was the hard part, but also the "worth it" part.

"Having happy thoughts?" someone asked. My

hand flew to that special signature on my orange cast. It was Michael Capezzi.

"I am," I said, but I really wanted to say, "I was."

"Where's that little sister of yours?" He looked around. "I forgot to wear my ankle protectors."

I laughed. The last time I saw Michael Capezzi, Sunny had told him that a classmate told her that every time a boy talked to your older sister, you were supposed to bite his ankles. I loved that he remembered that story. And that he remembered Sunny.

Batman ran up and tugged at Michael's arm.

"This is my little brother, Stanley," Michael said.

"I'm Batman," repeated the boy. "And she's Paintgirl."

Michael crossed his arms and stared down at the masked boy. And then in a very slow and steady voice, he said, "You are Stanley Capezzi. And this is Masha Sweet." My name sounded like a little song when he said it.

Robin ran up to us, his yellow bath towel flapping behind him. He threw his arms around me and cried, "Paintgirl! You're back."

"Your name is Patrick Capezzi," Michael said. "And her name is Masha Sweet."

"My name is Robin. And she's Paintgirl." Robin frowned.

"Michael," called a woman's voice. "Michael, Batman, Robin!"

"That's Mommy," said Batman. He and Robin looked at one another and then grinned up at their older brother.

Michael looked down at them and over at me with a shrug and said, "What can you do?"

"Protect your ankles and hope for the best," I said, pointing over at my little sister, who was still chatting with the judges. We looked back at one another and smiled.

"When you smile, your outside, it's pretty good," he said.

It took me a second to realize that Michael Capezzi was talking about my conversation with Alice in the graveyard—the one about wanting to be beautiful on the outside. But when I did, I felt stronger than fifty thousand superheroes.

Drawing Conclusions

Sunny packed her video equipment back into the two boxes while I watched. I wasn't going to help. I had done enough for Sunny Sweet for one day. She tried to put her trophy into one of the boxes, but it was too big to fit.

"Can you carry it?"

"No," I said, but I took it anyway and stuck it under my cast. The trophy was a weird roundish star stuck to a silver wave.

"It's an atom," Sunny said, pointing at the trophy.

"Who is Adam?"

"Not Adam. Atom," she said.

"Never mind," I said, "I don't care who it is."

I pulled out my phone and texted my mom that the fair was over and that, gasp, Sunny had won. I didn't put the word "gasp" into the text.

She immediately texted me back a series of big smiley faces, followed by a reminder to text her again when we got to Mrs. Song's. I texted that I would remember. And then before I hit Send, I put ten big smiley faces at the end of my message. I knew she would like that. It's stupid, but when I sent it, it made me smile just like the goofy yellow faces.

"Ready?" I asked, looking up from my phone.

"Almost," Sunny said, putting a bunch of wires into the box.

"Why does science have to come with so many wires?"

"What?" she asked.

"How did you do this, anyway?" I asked her. "Who set it all up?"

"Remember the envelope stuck to the side of this box?" she asked. "It had all the instructions for setting up my experiment, just in case I wasn't here to do it myself. I didn't know exactly how the experiment would happen since you were an unknown variable."

I actually liked the sound of being an unknown variable even if I wasn't sure what it meant. "But how did you know someone would do it?"

She shrugged. "I didn't really. I made an educated guess, called a hypothesis, that in a room full of scientists, someone would be curious enough to follow my instructions. But just in case, last night I also e-mailed all the instructions for setting up the experiment to Mrs. Terry, the head of the science fair." She threw her head back and laughed that hysterical evilgenius laugh of hers from deep within her skinny little neck. If it weren't for a group of kids that swarmed us at that very moment, my own educated guess is that I would have strangled her right then and there. The kids had pieces of paper and pens in their hands.

"Really?" I groaned. "Autographs?"

They glanced over at me for a second and then turned their full attention back toward Sunny Sweet. My phone buzzed with a text. Thank goodness. I turned my back on the science rock star and her groupies and checked my phone. I figured it was going to be another smiley face from my mom for the smiling faces I sent her, but instead, it was a text from Junchao. Finally!

Look to your left, it said.

I looked. And there was Junchao waving at me with some sort of space helmet on.

"Junchao!" I shouted, running over to her.

"Ni hao," she mouthed through the glass of her helmet.

"Where have you been?" I asked.

She took off her helmet. Her cheeks were pink, and her hair stood straight off her head.

"What?" she asked. "I can't hear a thing inside that helmet."

"Where were you all day?" I asked.

She winced at the sound of my voice, like it hurt her ears. "I was here at the fair," she said.

"Why didn't you pick up your phone?"

"Why are you shouting?" she asked.

"I'm not shouting," I said, quieting my voice. Maybe I was shouting.

"I'm sorry, Masha," she said. "I've been inside the helmet all day. My science experiment was recreating what space sounds like."

"What does space sound like?"

She handed me her helmet. I pulled off my hat and put her helmet on my head. And I heard absolutely nothing. No wonder she missed all my calls and texts.

Sunny walked over to us. She looked up at me and started to speak. I couldn't hear one word she said.

This was nice. I watched as Sunny pointed to the helmet and started talking to Junchao, probably about her experiment. Junchao answered. I just stood there enjoying the quiet until we were interrupted by a small woman who looked just like Junchao, except she was a lot older and her hair was a lot shorter. I didn't want to, but I took off the helmet.

"This is Masha and her little sister, Sunny," Junchao said to her mom. "Can we give them a ride home?"

"We certainly can," Mrs. Tao said. "On one condition . . ."

All three of us looked at Mrs. Tao

"That Sunny give Junchao her first-place trophy," she said. And then Mrs. Tao laughed. She had the same exact laugh as Junchao, and it was the best laugh ever. It sounded just like Santa Claus—ho-ho-ho.

Junchao pretended to reach for Sunny's trophy in my hands. Sunny grabbed it from me and hugged it to her chest. Junchao started laughing along with her mom. The sound of their "ho-ho-hoing" got me laughing too. Mrs. Tao and Junchao were obviously kidding, but Sunny still backed away from the three of us anyway.

When we got in the car, Junchao's mother told Sunny that she was a chemical engineer. Sunny forgot all about the trophy joke. She started right in with words like "fluid" and "flow" and "pumps" . . . all of which I didn't like the sound of. When Sunny got to listing her favorite chemicals—strontium, barium, radium—I asked Junchao to hand me her helmet.

I put it on and was officially in heaven. You could really hear nothing! I loved watching the telephone poles whisk by my eyes. One after another after another they slid past without the usual swooshing sound. We drove by a brown barking dog outside a big house on a corner—his snout snapped open and shut. But all I heard was silence.

The first thing I was going to do when we got home was to text my mom. The next thing I was going to do was to ask Mrs. Song if I could run across the yard to my house and take the longest shower ever in the history of showers. I was going to use the entire bottle of soap, if necessary, to scrub off all the dye and pottery dust and dried mud. And then I was going to eat about fifty-five million of Mrs. Song's dumplings. But there was one thing that I wasn't going to do, *and that was to tell my mother what happened today.* I would let her "ooh" and "aah" over Sunny's trophy, and I'd tell her that Junchao was there and that Mrs. Tao gave us a ride home, and maybe I'd tell her about this cool helmet—but that was it!

I glanced over at Sunny. Her mouth was like the dog barking . . . Her jaw was moving and moving and moving, but I heard nothing.

I wondered if Junchao would let me borrow this helmet for a few days. And because Junchao is my friend I'm going to make an educated guess, or to use Sunny's word, *hypothesize* that Junchao's answer is going to be yes.

I leaned back in my seat and closed my eyes. The car rocked me back and forth in comfortable silence. I was *finally* going home. My personal conclusion for the day? Science wasn't all bad.

Sunny Sweet Can So Get Lost

Y ou smell like a pickle."

"Yeah, I know," I said.

The little kid standing in front of me at the airport was not the first person to notice. It had been two months since Sunny had exploded red dye all over me and I *still* smelled like vinegar! Actually, I smelled like twenty-two bottles of vinegar because that is what it took to remove my evil little sister's latest science experiment from my skin.

"I like pickles," he said, licking his lips.

"I'm not a pickle."

I pulled my phone closer to my face to block the kid from my sight. My mother had filled our bathtub up with vinegar, and I had soaked in it for four straight hours. So maybe I was a pickle.

The kid didn't move.

"It's vinegar you smell," Sunny said, looking up from her book. "Vinegar is a liquid used in the process of preserving food, like cucumbers, which when preserved in vinegar are called pickles. This is why you think that my sister, Masha, smells like one."

The kid blinked at Sunny for a half second and then took off—hopping back to his mother along a row of attached chairs.

"Did you know . . . ," Sunny started.

"No," I said.

This didn't stop her. It never did. ". . . that the word 'vinegar' comes from the French words '*vin egre*,' which mean sour wine? So what you really smell like is sour wine."

"Can't you just let me smell like a pickle?" I asked.

My phone rang and I clicked it on. "Hi, Mom!"

"Hey, Masha. Are you and Sunny in Boston?"

"Yeah, we're here."

"Is the unaccompanied minor attendant with you?"

"Yes, Mom, I'm looking right at her and she's looking right back at me. Her name is Wendi, with an *i*. And no, you cannot talk to her. Sunny and I are fine."

"I wasn't even going to ask." She laughed. But I knew that she was. My mom was pretty nervous about Sunny and me flying out alone to meet our dad for summer vacation. We had to fly from Newark Airport in New Jersey up to Boston in Massachusetts. And from there, we'd fly all the way out west to South Dakota. My mom needed to fly to Russia to be with my grandmother for a surgery, so my father surprised Sunny and me with a trip to the Lone Creek Dude Ranch.

Sunny and I hadn't seen our dad since Christmas. But any butterflies swirling around my belly about not seeing him for so long were pretty much buried alive by the *awesometastic* news that I was going to get to ride a horse! My father sent us the brochure in the mail. On the cover was a shiny black horse running across a prairie. I made my mom rent *Black Beauty* that night, and I'd watched it every day since . . . twice a day on Sundays.

"I'm boarding soon," Mom said. She was still back in Newark Airport, where we left her that morning. "Let me say a quick hi to your sister."

I tried to hand Sunny my phone. She wouldn't take it. Instead, she put both her hands to her throat and pretended she couldn't speak. I rolled my eyes. "Sorry, Mom, she can't talk. She's got laryngitis."

My mom snorted with laugher. The little genius's new project these days was to follow my mother around as her mini personal secretary, writing her e-mails and picking up her phone calls. Whenever Sunny answered a call from a telemarketer, she would tell them that my mom had laryngitis and couldn't talk. My mom thought it was the funniest thing ever, especially when Sunny explained how the larynx and trachea worked to the poor marketing people.

"Well, tell your sister I said I love her. And that I love the group texts you guys are sending to me. They are so cute."

"Group texts?" I repeated, glancing over at Sunny. Sunny didn't take her eyes off her book, but I could tell by how she stared at one spot on the page that she heard me.

"That reminds me," she continued. "I got the strangest e-mail from your father."

"An e-mail from Dad? What did he say?" I asked. "Was it about my horse?"

Sunny put her book down and swiped at my phone. I batted her off like a fly.

"Masha Sweet," my mother said, sighing. When my mom calls me this, I know she's serious. And she had been calling me this a lot in the last few weeks. "Your father is not buying you a horse. I know he said that he had a surprise for you and Sunny, but I'm sure the surprise is *not a horse*. I wish you would stop hoping because you're just going to be disappointed."

"Well what exactly did he say?" I moaned. I wasn't going to stop hoping for my horse. Hope was all I had. Anyway, what else could the surprise be? He was taking us to a dude ranch, and he had made a big deal of a having a surprise for Sunny and me. I don't see how my mom could think that I *wasn't* getting a horse!

"He said that he knows. And not to worry," my mother said.

"What?" I asked.

Sunny tried to snatch the phone from me again. I swooped away from her and into the seat on the other side of me. Unfortunately, that seat happened to be occupied by a man reading a newspaper. The man cleared his throat, warning me, I guess, to calm down.

I smiled, thinking about how the man had just treated me like a normal kid, using the normal way that adults do to signal kids to cut it out. And this is because, except for smelling slightly like a garden salad, I *was* a normal kid. It hadn't been that long ago that Sunny had glued a million plastic flowers to my head and I had to have my head shaved. Or that I had been covered in red dye when Sunny had exploded a bottle of ketchup all over me so she could win a science fair. But today my hair was looking pretty cute in a bob. And today my skin was splotch-free. In fact, today dinky Dr. Frankenstein had not done one terrible thing to me.

I felt a tiny pinch in my stomach at that last thought. I looked over at Sunny. She was busy with her phone.

"Oh, I'm boarding," my mom said, breathless. She always got so excited when it was time to get on a plane. A big wave of missing her broke over me. She was getting on a plane and we were getting on a plane, but we weren't getting on the same plane.

"Kisses and hugs," she said. "I'll give Babushka all

your love, and you guys have a great time with your father. Tell Sunny the same. Oh, and tell her that I loved finding her travel safety plan in my carry-on." She gave a tiny shriek of joy. "The organization chart of emergency numbers and addresses was terrific! And the detailed outline of contingency emergency plans for natural disasters and power outages was really above and beyond, even for your little sister."

Again I looked over at Sunny. She was still playing with her phone. I didn't like hearing about this stuff . . . the safety plan and the texts. That pinch in my stomach was growing into an actual ache. Sunny was up to something. I looked around. Everything looked okay. We were at our gate. Wendi with an *i* was constantly staring over at us from the ticket counter as if we might disappear at any moment. I had my ticket information and ID around my neck. Sunny had hers. I just wish my mom hadn't said that thing about Sunny, because one thing I knew to be true: *nothing was above and beyond my little sister.*

"A gazillion kisses right back, Mom. I love you, love you, love you," I told her.

She smacked me a real kiss through the phone and then she was gone. I took a deep breath filled with wishing that my mother were here with us or that we were there with her. No . . . wait. I didn't want to be going to Russia to watch my grandmother's hip get fixed—I wanted to be going to the Lone Creek Dude Ranch to ride horses!

The sight of Sunny's skinny little fingers bouncing about on her phone keys caught my attention. "What are you doing?" I asked.

"What?"

"What are you doing?"

I looked closer at her phone. "Are you checking Mom's e-mails?" My heart fluttered. "Check the one from Dad. See if he said anything about my horse."

"I hate horses," she said, not taking her eyes off her screen.

I leaned back in my airport chair and closed my eyes. *I love horses.*

The vision of my horse shimmered into my head. He was a dark chocolate brown with a long black mane. His eyes were huge and kind. His coat shone from all of my brushing. We walked together, his nose nuzzling my ear. And then I jumped onto to his back and we rode along cliffs overlooking the ocean.

Wendi with an *i* interrupted my dream.

"We're going to be boarding soon," she said, and then I watched as she turned and walked back over to the tiny ticket counter to chat with the other flight attendants at the entrance to the gate. Over the counter in dotted red lit-up letters it said PORTLAND.

"Hey, Sunny, I remember mom saying that the airport we are flying into is like Sioux Falls or something," I said, pointing at the sign.

Sunny glanced up at the sign. Then she hopped out of her seat. "I have to go to the bathroom."

"You just went."

"Um," she said, "I have to go again."

I didn't want to go to the bathroom again. I wanted to go back to dreaming my wonderful horse dreams. We weren't supposed to go anywhere alone, even the bathroom. So if I called Wendi with an *i,* I would have to go too. I looked up at Wendi with an *i.* She was bent over the desk writing something. "Just go," I said. "But hurry up."

I immediately went back to dreaming about Oscar or Charlie, which both sounded like solid horse names. But I also kind of liked the more horsey-sounding names, like Thunder and Black Cloud. I got my phone back out and went to this website I'd found with a ton of pictures of horses and started scrolling through them—white horses, brown horses, white and brown horses, horses running in groups, horses running through long grass, horses jumping, horses with giant hooves, horses pulling carts, horses, horses, horses . . .

The quietness poked at me. I looked up to see the last few people at the gate heading onto the plane.

"Sunny?" I looked around me. "Sunny!" I yelped.

I jumped out of my seat. Where was Sunny? Where was Wendi with an *i*? How long had I been looking at horses? I ran down the wide airport hall and into the bathroom. "Sunny!" I called. There was no answer, but I did hear something . . . It was Sunny's voice in my head. *I hate horses.*

All of a sudden an avalanche of the things Sunny had been doing and saying lately rolled over the top of me—Sunny asking over and over why we couldn't just go to our old house in Pennsylvania to see Dad, or Sunny begging to go with my mom to Babushka's in Saint Petersburg. And then there was all her complaining about the dude ranch and how she didn't like square dancing and how they would probably only be serving ribs, which she couldn't eat because my six-year-old sister had now become a vegetarian. Finally, in my head I heard her say, "I have to go to the bathroom," and I knew . . . *she didn't really have to go to the bathroom.*

Holy frozen ravioli . . . Sunny Sweet was gone!

I gave a short little howl and ran out of the bathroom and straight into Wendi with an *i*.

"Oh my gosh!" Wendi with an *i* cried, almost hugging me. "Where have you been?"

"Uh . . . uh," I said.

She locked arms with me and pulled me toward the gate. I stumbled along next to her, searching every face in the airport for Sunny's.

"My sister," I huffed, "is los—" I stopped. Sunny Sweet was gone, but she wasn't lost. Sunny Sweet didn't get lost. You had to *not* know where you were to be lost, and wherever Sunny was at this moment, she knew exactly where she was! I thought about what my mother said on the phone, about some sort of group text that Sunny sent. And that safety thing that she put in my mom's bag. Then I thought about Sunny taking all of my mom's phone calls and writing all her e-mails for the last couple of months. I didn't know the reason why she was doing these things, but I did know that there was a reason. She was definitely up to something. And this time I wasn't going to be a part of it.

"Time to get on that plane," Wendi with an *i* said, pointing toward the flight attendant waiting at the gate.

I took one last look around. *I bet Sunny is watching me right this minute. I bet she is wondering what I'll do next.* I wasn't going to let her do this to me again. I thought about Oscar/Charlie/Thunder/Black Cloud. I wanted my horse. That decided it.

Sunny Sweet can so get lost! But I certainly wasn't getting lost with her.

I turned and walked down the tiny airplane hallway. I was free, free, free of Sunny Sweet forever . . .
or for at least three weeks, which was good enough.
Plus I'd have two whole seats on the plane so I could
stretch out and eat and . . . what was I doing? *Sunny!*

I swung around. There stood Wendi with an *i* with
her arms crossed in front of her, blocking my path.
"My little sister. She's . . ." That's when I heard Sunny's
voice coming from behind me. "On the plane?" I finished. I turned and hurried through the spaceship-
looking portal of the plane. There was Sunny Sweet,
standing with the pilot telling jokes.

"Why did the chicken cross the Möbius strip?" she
said.

"Why?" laughed the pilot.

"To get to the same side."

They both cracked up laughing.

"Hey, Masha, get it?" she asked. "Because a Möbius
strip only has one side."

"I get it," I sighed, even though I didn't get it. I
never got it. Even when I thought I got it, I didn't get
it. I thought Sunny Sweet was lost. She wasn't. I

thought Sunny Sweet was up to something. But she wasn't. I guess my evil-genius little sister really did like explaining laryngitis to poor, unsuspecting tele-marketers and making up organization charts and detailed safety plans.

"Hey, Sunny," the pilot said. He already knew her name. "Do you want to announce our departure?" He held out a walkie-talkie-looking thing to her.

"I'm going to the bathroom," I told Sunny. "Be in the aisle seat when I get back. It's my turn to sit by the window."

I trudged down the aisle, trying to get a minute of my life without my little sister in it. Sunny's voice followed me the entire way. "Ladies and gentlemen, please take your seats as we get ready to depart," she said. "Please turn off all electronic devices, such as cell phones and computers."

I closed the bathroom door and pulled out my phone. I had a text from my friend Junchao. She was spending her summer vacation at some horrible science camp, although she seemed pretty excited about it. Junchao knew I was going to a dude ranch, but I didn't tell her about Oscar/Charlie/Thunder/Black Cloud because I didn't want to ruin her happiness about only getting to go to a lousy camp when I was getting a horse! Her text said:

Don't ride off into the sunset!

I texted back my usual.

Ho-ho-ho.

Junchao was as tiny as a mouse but had the biggest, Santa Claus–iest laugh you ever heard. Every time I heard it, I had to laugh, too.

Sunny's voice blared through speakers in the bathroom, giving me the local time we'd be landing. Even in here I couldn't get away from her.

I texted my friend Alice good-bye and told her to have a great time. She was taking a family trip to Florida. A foundation gave it to them because of Alice's spina bifida. As much as Alice hated being treated differently because of her spine not working right and because she needed a wheelchair, she got over it real quick when the words "Disney World" got mentioned. I might have been totally green with jealousy if I weren't getting my very own horse!

"Preparing for takeoff . . ." came Sunny's voice again.

They better not be letting Sunny Sweet fly this plane! I opened up the door and hurried back to our row. Sunny was sitting in the aisle seat. Thank goodness. I leaped over her to get to the window. I buckled up and looked out at the bustle of the airport tarmac. Time to chill out and dream about trotting and cantering and galloping. The plane moved away from the gate. The engine fired up beneath us, and we began to race down the runway. I was rushing toward my horse!

"Hello, this is your captain speaking," said a friendly voice over the intercom.

"That's Bob," Sunny said.

"Our time of departure is 6:32 p.m. Eastern Standard Time. And we should be landing in Portland, Maine, just around 7:15 p.m."

Portland, Maine?

I looked over at Sunny. She stared down at the page in her book, but I knew she was seeing me seeing her.

"What did Bob mean by Portland, M—" I couldn't even finish the sentence because I finally got it. I got all of it. Playing secretary for my mom, faking laryngitis, sending group texts, and writing up emergency plans. I got it. Sunny Sweet was getting lost—and she was taking me with her! We were not on our way to Lone Creek Dude Ranch.

"But the tickets? And Wendi with an *i*?" I whispered.

She put down her book and looked at me. "Good planning," she said.

Oscar/Charlie/Thunder/Black Cloud. Noooooooo!

I struggled to open my seat belt. I was getting out of here.

"Keep that buckled," a flight attendant hissed from a few seats away.

"I need to . . . !" I shouted.

"After takeoff," she said, not letting me finish. But it was too late, and I knew it.

The plane lifted off the ground and into the air. I fell back into my seat and watched with wide-open eyes as the world grew smaller and smaller beneath us.

"But why?" I asked. I could barely look at her.

Sunny pulled a brochure from her backpack and put it on my lap.

I looked down.

"Math camp?" I shouted over the engine of the plane.

**INQUIRE
INVESTIGATE
INVENT**

*Blending Science, Technology, Engineering,
and Merriment since 1952.*

**Welcome to the Newton
Camp of Mathematics!**

"Yes!" Sunny giggled. "It's going to be so great. They have a whole series on robotics, and one on mechanical engineering, and one on environmental sustainability, and one on genetics . . ." She had to stop to breathe. "We will actually get to genetically modify cells to smell like other stuff, like flowers or rotten eggs or anything. And look!" she said, her little hands shaking with excitement as she opened the brochure on my lap and pointed at a heading.

I read:

FUN WITH DNA

"We're going to get to extract DNA from our very own cells!" she squealed, snatching the brochure from my lap and flipping through it. "Just think, Masha, space rovers and astrophysics and new geometric worlds and . . ."

"Horses," I choked. "What about horses?"

"Horses?" Sunny snorted—her nose now buried deep within the brochure. "I doubt it."

I started to feel woozy. I couldn't breathe. I needed air. I groped the seat around me.

"What are you doing?"

"What does it look like I'm doing?" I snapped. "I'm looking for an oxygen mask."

"Why?" she asked. "The aircraft's pressurization is fine. Look at this." She poked the brochure back in my face. "We gather our DNA by spitting into a cup."

I shoved the brochure away from me and pressed

my entire body against the window of the plane to get as far away from Sunny Sweet as I could. We were passing through a bunch of fluffy white clouds. *How could she do this?*

"I'm calling Mom as soon as we land," I said. I felt like I might throw up.

"A typical commercial flight between New York and Saint Petersburg, Russia, is approximately nine hours and five minutes," she said. "But of course, the exact time depends on wind speeds."

"Then I'm calling Dad."

"He went to Thailand," she said.

"What do you mean he went to Thailand?" I put my head in my hands and groaned. I was definitely going to throw up. "It's really over. We're really lost."

"'Not all those who wander are lost,'" Sunny said, flipping through her dumb brochure. "That's a quote from J. R. R. Tolkien. He wrote *Lord of the Rings*."

"Here's a quote for you," I said. "'Annoying little sisters who wander often get lost when they are shoved into very deep wells. Masha Sweet wrote that." I smiled.

Acknowledgments

Cross the river in a crowd and the crocodile
won't eat you. —African proverb

Caroline Abbey • Shari Becker

Alice Carpenter • Christopher Carpenter

Leslie Caulfield • Heather Demetrios-Fehst

Kim Griswell • Helle Henriksen

Marileta Robinson • Max Rottersman

Kerry Sparks • Carolyn Yoder • Junchao Yu